A Dragon, a Gargoyle, and a Faery Make a Wish

Nicole DragonBeck
and Lisa Barry

Book Cover designed by Nicole DragonBeck

Witching Hour Publishing, Inc.

eBook ISBN: 978-1-943121-80-9
Print ISBN: 978-1-943121-82-3

Contents

Chapter 1 - Aiden
A Once In A Lifetime Opportunity

Wednesday, 19 August 2015, 4:52 PM (Dublin - Headquarters of the Keepers of the Peace and Order of Chroniclers)

Detective Aiden Moss stared at the screen, finding himself at a rare loss for words. How to tell the truth, without *really* giving away what maybe could be considered the *whole* truth?

The troll *had* resisted the arrest, but when the mermaid - who the detectives had *thought* was their informant, but had really been in league with the troll and double-crossing them - had dumped a thousand gallons of seawater containing a rather large, irate kraken on them at their ambush...well, things had gone to hell in a handbasket rather suddenly. Torloch Doyle's quick thinking had saved them and contained the situation without *too* much collateral damage, but Director Arthur Warren wouldn't necessarily see it that way.

What had Warren said last time? Aiden thought, trying to remember the exact words that had come out of the infuriated leprechaun's mouth. "*Doyle, when it was raining brains, you had your umbrella up. The next time you put one toe out of line, I'm going to put you on permanent administration duty*". Or something like that anyway. The leprechaun had a habit of making threats that he and everyone else later forgot.

Aiden's fingers hovered over the keyboard, trying to sort necessary details from anything the Director didn't really need to know. Intense hazel eyes were narrowed at the not-yet-written report, and dark, straight hair lay neatly to his shoulders.

"Five o'clock, time to go."

The dragon didn't move his eyes from the screen, not even when his partner Torloch cleared his throat loudly across the room, and repeated what he'd just said, as though it hadn't been heard the first time.

"I have two more items to address here," Aiden said, fighting to keep his concentration.

"Which you can do *tomorrow*," the gargoyle replied, and pointed at the clock. "The show starts in thirty minutes."

Torloch was dressed in his customary all-black ensemble, his leather jacket and messy brown hair ready to make at least a few girls go weak at the knees when he flashed them his charming grin. Aiden wore slacks and a jacket, and he knew that he would feel overdressed at the event, but he was used to that by now.

"Remind me again, what exactly did you do with the kraken?" Aiden asked, deleting the last thing he had written. *Panthéa, this was annoying.*

"I put it in containment, just like we discussed."

"And you filled out the form I told you to?"

"Form?" Torloch scratched his head as though he had never heard of such a thing. "What form?"

"The F-99," Aiden said patiently. "Which you have to log in order to put a live creature into containment."

Torloch nodded with a very thoughtful expression on his face.

Aiden sighed. "The *same* form that we'll need to release the creature back to the wild, and prove that the measures that were taken were, in fact, in proportion to and warranted by the situation at hand."

"You know, when I pulled you out of the tentacles and saved your scaly hide from a watery death, I *don't* recall needing a form for that," the gargoyle commented, and Aiden put his face in his hands.

"And another thing," Torloch continued, and the dragon looked up. "The show now starts in *twenty-five* minutes."

"And Warren will have my hide if this report isn't turned in," Aiden said. "How exactly are you planning on saving me from *that*?"

"If you're going to be a killjoy all night, I could just go by myself," Loch said. "I know of at least three lovely women downstairs who would kill for a chance to see a live performance by Uaithne."

Aiden rolled his eyes, but he knew the gargoyle was right. Getting a ticket to the performance of the famous harpist - a legend from the old days of Ireland and court musician for the Dagda himself - *was* a once in a lifetime opportunity, even when your lifetime spanned centuries like that of both the dragons and the gargoyles.

Torloch raised his brows and gestured at the door with an impatient expression. Aiden threw his hands up and saved the progress on his computer then shut it down, leaving just the office screensaver - a black shield with wand and sword crossed over the three leaves symbolic of the Fae Courts. The dragon grabbed his jacket and hurried through the crowded hallways of the KPOC Headquarters. He couldn't remember the last time he had left work early enough to have to duck and dodge the other agents and staff also leaving for the night.

The dragon nodded and mumbled "good evening" to the group of witches he passed, the elf wheeling the wagon with post and packages, and the trio of giggling interns who chorused "Hi, Detective Doyle!" as the gargoyle passed.

Aiden thought it would be too cruel to tell them they needed at least another twenty years before they would appeal to the mature tastes of the gargoyle. As their adolescent attachment was harmless, he kept his tongue, but he couldn't stop the slight shake of his head.

Aiden had taken less than two steps out of the wide double-doors of the side entrance and into the car park when the first drops of rain landed on his face, and he blinked them away.

"I hope this clears up in the next fifteen minutes," Aiden said.

"Don't worry," Torloch said. "Uaithne has a whole team of warlocks setting up his stage. You'll be dry and comfy, I promise."

"How do you know so much about that?" Aiden said.

"Have you never heard of a groupie?" Torloch grinned at him, and Aiden shook his head in disbelief.

The gargoyle stopped dead, staring ahead.

"What's the matter?" the dragon asked, peering around his friend.

"What is that?" Torloch pointed at something in the distance.

"That's your car," Aiden said, glancing at the purple Cuda.

"No, gobshite, *next* to the car," the gargoyle said.

Aiden squinted into the distance, and saw the small figure in the pink jacket and bright yellow overshoes, carrying something under one arm, dancing about in the rain with happy squeals.

"It's a child," Aiden said. "Not a terrorist."

"It better not damage my baby," Torloch said.

The dragon rolled his eyes and walked over. The little girl's neck stretched back to look up at him with big blue eyes wide in surprise. He knelt down and smiled at her. After a moment's hesitation, she smiled back, and held out the teddy bear for a silent introduction. The bear had black button eyes, and a pink and yellow spotted ribbon around its neck.

"Hello," Aiden said.

"Hi," she said shyly, and Aiden frowned but quickly smoothed the expression off his face so he didn't scare her.

He waved the gargoyle closer.

"Uh, Torloch?" Aiden said softly.

"Yes?"

"This is not a fae child. She's human."

"And?"

"So, how did she get past the wards?"

Torloch opened his mouth to reply, then frowned and looked out to the green of Phoenix Park, beyond the ancient and very strong spells that kept the Headquarters of the Keepers of the Peace and the Order of Chroniclers safe from Outside eyes, like those of the little human girl standing in front of them.

"Yes, how did she manage that?" the gargoyle asked.

Chapter 2 - Loch

No Signal Here in Nowhereville

Wednesday, 19 August 2015, 5:16 PM (Dublin - Headquarters of the Keepers of the Peace and Order of Chroniclers)

Loch rubbed his chin, an unusual gesture for the gargoyle, but he was genuinely perplexed that the small human had crossed the heavily warded lines to enter the KPOC headquarters. Sure, it was just the carpark, but still, it was the carpark *in* the KPOC headquarters.

Not to mention the fact that she was *very* close to his classic car and swinging that bear around like a balloon in the wind. The bear itself wouldn't do any damage, but those button eyes...his eyes narrowed and he took a step closer to see how he could increase the distance between the girl and his car.

He waved his hands in a shooing motion and the girl frowned at him.

"Torloch, she's not a fly."

"Yes, but-"

A loud squeal made Loch pause with a heavy frown. The youngster shot forward with a broad smile, away from his car thankfully, and rushed toward the small garden tucked to the side of the car park, conveniently interspersed with benches for a break from the office or quiet lunch.

Aiden and Loch watched as the girl giggled and skipped along, periodically reaching forward as though she was trying to catch something. It was then that Loch noticed the small flutter of wings and flash of gold, just ahead of her.

"Pixie!" Aiden announced and rushed forward.

"Feck!" Loch breathed out as he followed Aiden's lead and surged toward the edge of the garden. His eyes moved to the green of Phoenix Park, beyond the main wards, to the gathering swirl of purple and teal mist, dancing with silver sparkles. "A, there's a portal opening there!"

"I see it!"

The faint tinkle of a pixie laugh shot fear down Loch's spine.

"That little-"

He rushed forward tripping over an overgrown vine but catching himself before falling to his knees. Aiden was a few steps ahead until a tree branch seemed to appear from nowhere and whack him in the face. The dragon muttered some vocabulary that didn't generally leave his mouth before moving forward again.

Loch was almost there. He dived for the ground, hoping to grab the girl before she reached the door to the Faeways, but he hadn't anticipated the rain turning the ground slick and treacherous, his feet shot out from under him. He slid through the grass at great speed, managing to scoop up the girl as he went. She shrieked and began hitting him on the head with her bear while hollering "bad wolf".

The gargoyle could hear Aiden calling his name and he tried to maneuver the girl, the wet grass and his large body all while heading directly toward the portal.

"Aiden!" he called before he flipped to his back, changed his free arm to that of his gargoyle form and pressed his claws into the soft dirt bringing him to a slow halt.

Breathing out a sigh, he let the girl jump away from him with one last whack to his head. The groundskeeper would *not* be happy with the mess he had made of the lawn, but disaster had been averted. Aiden's shadow would have been what clued him in to the dragon's approach but it was the soft chuckle that did it. Loch lifted himself onto his elbows and glared.

"Where were you during this-"

Aiden's eyes doubled and he lunged past Loch and dove after the girl as she walked straight into the portal which had moved to intercept her. Loch jumped up and twisted in time to grab the bottom of Aiden's jacket as he was half dragged and half chased Aiden through the portal entrance.

They found themselves in a wide, misty hallway of colorful doors in all shapes and sizes. Aiden scooped up the child and she let out a high pitched wail. Loch watched Aiden's brows shoot up in distress as he looked to the gargoyle. Loch grinned. Making sure he was in the girl's line of sight, he stumbled. The keening stopped. Loch took another step and fell into the wall with a grunt. A small giggle. Lifting his right arm and leg and then switching to the other side, he did a silly dance in the strange hallway. The girl laughed and started waving the bear around.

Changing the dance, Loch looked at Aiden who was desperately trying to contain his own laughter.

"Let it out, you stick in the mud,"

Aiden snorted, a fume of smoke leaving his nostrils. The girl reached up to catch it before poking the dragon in the nose effectively erasing any mirth he might have harbored. She now seemed content to sit in Aiden's arms, and the two detectives turned their attention to their predicament.

"I don't like to travel the Faeways without a fae present." Aiden said quietly. "It's far too easy to get lost."

"One thousand percent agreed," Loch nodded as he did a two step. Or what he thought might be a two step. "So, do we pick a door? Or see if someone else shows up?"

"I'm worried that we're in *her* concept."

Loch sighed. "I did have that thought. Maybe if you put her down she'll find the right door?"

He thought about the almost sentient actions of the Faeways, more like a computer waiting for an order but from the mind. What it would do with a child's mind wasn't something he wanted to contemplate very much right now.

"You think she'd know which door is the one she needs?" the dragon asked, looking uncertain.

Loch shrugged. "If she got us here in the first place, I wouldn't see why not."

Aiden let out a long breath before leaning down and depositing the girl onto the tiled floor, and followed with a little shooing motion. Loch frowned. When they had first arrived, the floor had been a shiny white and now it was black and white tile, like an old diner. The girl started down the hall, Aiden and Loch close behind. Something flittered in Loch's peripheral, and he watched as a zip of sparkles flew by, tousling the girl's hair before stopping in front of a yellow door and vanishing.

"Oh, this can't be good," Loch started to run past the others towards the yellow door.

He opened the door and peered inside before doing anything else. A gust of stale air washed over him as he looked out at a black chasm of nothingness. He closed the door.

"That is not our way out," he commented, rubbing the back of his head as the little girl walked past him and wrinkled her nose at him.

He frowned and cursed.

"Language," Aiden reminded him.

"Bollux," Loch muttered. "I'm missing my show."

"Sorry about that, mate."

Loch sniffed as he pulled his phone from his pocket. "No signal here in nowhereville."

They continued to follow the girl down the hall as she passed door after door. They went past tall thin ones with frosted windows, great oak doors with studded metal bindings, round doors with periwinkle trim or gold tracery, and ancient doors with iron knockers in the shape of monsters or angels. The child paused in front of a fairly normal looking green one and smiled as she started whacking it with her bear, pointing with her other hand at the lever handle she could not reach. Aiden pulled her away from the door, causing a great disturbance in the soundwaves around them, and Loch gritted his teeth at her whining as he opened the door to check it out.

The first thing he noted was the supremely fantastic smell of peppers, cumin, fried meat and fresh corn tortillas. He looked over the yellow washed hallway beyond, spying the public jacks and what resembled a kitchen door with windows. He turned a wide grin at Aiden.

"Hungry?"

Chapter 3 - Aiden
A Proper Little Monster

Wednesday, 19 August 2015, 8:42 PM (A Mexican Restaurant - somewhere on Earth, hopefully)

How Torloch could think about food at a time like this was beyond Aiden.

"I would really just like to get out of the Faeways, thank you very much," the dragon said.

Torloch gestured with his usual theatrical insouciance, and Aiden kept a firm grip on the child's hand as he walked through the door. It would *not* do to have her lost in the ways, especially as they had no idea how they had gotten in or out. The gargoyle nodded politely at a woman gaping at the three people who had stepped out of thin air as she was eating her dessert. She closed her mouth and looked away, shaking her head and muttering to herself.

The restaurant was paneled in wood, and the chairs were all different colors, the tables all different sizes. A door with stairs leading to the ground floor was visible at the back. Pink boxes of wine stacked in the corner, against a pastel chevron-patterned wall accent. One customer was digging into a large cast iron pan of seafood stew - lobster and mussels and crab in rice - while another had a plate of ribs and chips.

"Where are we?" Aiden asked.

Torloch pulled out his phone, and his eyebrows went up. He showed the GPS screen to the dragon.

"?" Aiden said, immediately feeling queasy.

It was purely in his head, but traveling any distance in the Faeways made him want to lose his last meal.

"El Boni Grill and Tapas," Torloch replied, looking around with shining eyes as he plucked a laminated card from a nearby table. "Should we get some food?"

"The menu is in Spanish," Aiden said.

"But I understand *hamburguesa,*" the gargoyle said with a grin. "*Hamburguesa simple, hamburguesa completa,* and *hamburguesa doble.*"

He knelt down with an encouraging smile at the girl. "Do you want something to eat? *Hamburguesa?*"

She nodded with a wide smile. "Boogers."

"See? She understands too," Torloch said with a triumphant look at Aiden, and went off to find someone to take his dinner order.

The dragon urged the little girl over to the nearest empty table and took a seat beside her. *This was an absolute nightmare,* the dragon thought.

He took out his phone, and started a detailed text to the Director, citing the proper Codex subsections, and requesting leave to address the situation with haste yet discretion. Torloch came up and leaned over his shoulder, then snorted.

"Dude, you're not really going to send that, are you?" the gargoyle asked. "Relax mate, we're not on Mars. We're just going to grab a bite, and then in just a blink we'll be back in Dublin."

"We'll be back in Dublin?" Aiden repeated, irritated both by his partner's cavalier attitude, and the time taken to compose the now useless text. "Really? How do you suppose we're going to manage that? We can't use the Faeways."

"We'll fly," the gargoyle looked at him as if he were daft.

"And we'll just leave her here then?" Aiden said, deleting each word he'd carefully selected with much reluctance, and hoping he didn't regret listening to the gargoyle on this.

"I was thinking we'd take her with us," Torloch said with an eye roll, drumming his fingers on the table and looking about.

"We cannot just shift and fly a child across a *country* and the *sea*," Aiden said. "Do you have any idea how many regulations that would be breaking?"

"No, but I have the feeling you're going to tell me."

"Torloch, this is serious."

"Okay, so we take a plane back to Dublin, like *normal people*," Toloch said, holding his hands out as if he were surrendering. "You know, some humans are aware of the fae world. Maybe she would be one of the good ones."

He reached out and ruffled her hair, and she grinned and cooed at him, *bad wolf* apparently now *friendly wolf.*

"Torloch, you're still not taking this seriously," Aiden said. "This is *bad*. This whole situation smells of something nefarious."

"Maybe not," the gargoyle countered. "Maybe she just wandered off when her parents were looking at the deer, and has some fae blood in her."

"I don't think so," Aiden said.

"What, don't tell me dragon's have x-ray vision that allows them to do DNA tests with a glance?" Toloch said. "How could you *possibly* know that?"

"I don't know that, I'm making a reasoned deduction," Aiden said. "*Even* if she was fully fae-blooded, she's not opening doors *and* bringing a dragon and a gargoyle through the

Faeways at this age. Where did that pixie she was chasing go, exactly?"

Torloch scratched his head, and then shrugged. "You have a point there."

"Yes, I do. More than one, actually," the dragon held out his hand and began to count off on his fingers. "She's a child, so *someone* brought her to Headquarters, *past* the wards. No three-year-old is wandering in Phoenix Park alone, fae or otherwise. She wasn't crying, or distraught. She was happy, and felt safe. What does that mean? I have no idea, but if we're going to unravel this case, we have to put our detective hats on."

"You want me to go get my trenchcoat too?" the gargoyle asked, then held up his hand to ward off Aiden's sharp retort. "You're right, you're right. I just need some food in me to help the old mind function properly."

Aiden looked around, wondering why the food was taking so long. In the corner of the restaurant, an iridescent fuchsia sparkle caught his eye.

"We've got company," the dragon said, and Torloch turned and sighed.

"How the feck does he *always* find us?"

"Hiya Rudy," Aiden said, nodding at the new arrival now standing at their tiny table.

The faery had his glamor in full force, and all anyone would see was a short, dark haired man with a childish face, and dark eyes that would sometimes seem to flash purple, which would quickly be written off to a trick of the light.

"Hi guys!" Rudy said in his squeaky, excited voice, and waved as if he were across the street.

"We see you Rudy," Torloch said. "What do you want?"

"I felt you guys come through the Faeways," he said.

"Well, that doesn't make me feel uncomfortable at all," the dragon growled. "Isn't that a bit voyeuristic, Rudy?"

"It's not like *that*," Rudy said. "I thought you might need some help."

"We don't, thanks Rudy," Torloch said. "Now bugger off."

"No, I *really* think you guys might need some help," the faery prince insisted, and looked around.

"Excuse me," he said to a trio sitting at the closest table. "Are you using this chair? No? Mind if I-okay, okay, thank you. Thank you."

He dragged the bright red chair over, and suddenly the rather small table just got uncomfortably crowded. "Look guys, I think I should stick around-OW!"

The faery almost left the ground in shock, and his glamor faltered, revealing his true face and semi-translucent wings for a second. The girl had grabbed onto a wing, and was yanking happily, twisting the delicate purple membrane with fingers that were much stronger than they looked.

"Get her off of me!" Rudy yelped, and Loch gently pried her fingers away while unsuccessfully trying to stifle his laughter.

"She's a proper little monster," the faery said with a pained pout. "I don't know what's going on in his thick head, that he thinks he can get a ransom for returning *that*. I bet you they pay him to *keep* her."

His eyes widened when both the dragon and the gargoyle grabbed an arm, and leveled very intense glares at him.

"Alright, Rudy, spill, and *quickly*," Aiden said, not liking this development one bit, and liking that it came from Ruaidhrí Mac Ríona, Unseelie prince and royal pain in the arse even less.

"Yes, what is this about a ransom?" Loch added. "And who is *him?*"

Chapter 4 - Loch
Anytime Now, Faery

Wednesday, 19 August 2015, 9:51 PM (El Boni restaurant in Spain)

Despite the serious questions posed upon Rudy, Loch was beside himself with delight when their meals arrived at that moment, interrupting his answer as the plates were placed in the middle of the table. He looked over the fare, and swore he heard an angelic choir serenading them from above - serrano ham and cream cheese cachopo, cecina and goat croquettes, peppered codfish, spicy potatoes, a burger and bowl of chips.

Aiden raised a brow, but Loch just smiled and passed out empty plates. He put a croquette and some chips on one plate and slid it to the little girl who stopped squirming to inspect it. Even one handed, since the other held firmly onto Rudy's arm, Loch filled his plate from the selection and forked several mouthfuls before continuing the grilling of the faery.

"So what were you saying, Roo?"

"Oh, come on guys. Come on. You know I messed up, can't we leave it there?"

"No," Loch stated before holding his fork out, loaded with cachopo to Aiden. "Dude, this is the best I've ever had. Who knew?"

Aiden cocked a brow and shook his head. He picked up his own fork and waved it before him, the other also holding firmly onto Rudy's arm. "I'm quite sure I can handle my own meal."

They both turned and looked at the little girl. She was giving herself one bite of a chip and then serving her bear a bite of chip. Loch watched as half of the contents of her plate rolled down the bear and onto the floor before turning back to the faery. The gargoyle smiled broadly.

"Well, Rudy, looks like you're finally catching on to what spy work is all about."

Rudy stopped struggling, and gave him a suspicious squint. "I am?"

Torloch nodded his head, with a very serious expression, one Aiden would be proud of. "Absolutely. Like a natural. Drop a few hints, be subtle, give your contact the information without outing yourself as the snitch. Pretty impressive."

"It is?" The faery was nodding along with Loch now. "Yeah, that's right guys, I'm really getting the hang of this."

Loch drummed his fingers on the table. *Anytime now, faery.* He didn't look at Aiden but he could feel the dragon's amusement across the table as he probably very grudgingly ate the meal he hadn't wanted, but since food really did increase mental prowess, he really didn't have a choice. Loch took another bite of the croquette and nearly swooned. He would have to come here again someday, under more favorable circumstances, and *definitely* with more favorable company.

"Oh, r i g h t," Rudy finally cooed. "Right, right. So the far darrig family likes getting rewards for their sinister deeds, ya know?"

"Who exactly?" Loch tried not to show his lack of patience in his face though he was entertained by the fact that the fairy didn't have nearly the hold on this whole subtly dropping-clues-investigation business that he thought he did.

"The Farrell clan?" Rudy looked at the ceiling, insinuating a guess though he just dropped a huge clue. "From up in County Longford?"

"Ah, right mate," Loch took a sip of his water and winked at Aiden.

"The Red Caped," Aiden murmured, "They are not the kindest lot."

Loch snorted. "Distant cousins of Warren, little feckers."

"I think not," Aiden was affronted on Warren's behalf. "The far darrig are the exact opposite of the leprechauns."

Loch shrugged. "*Exact* opposite? That's a bit of a stretch, mate."

Aiden shook his head as he cut the hamburger in two and put half of it on his plate along with some of the codfish.

"So, who's the kid?" Loch asked, tossing up a chip and catching it in his mouth resulting in a pleased giggle from the child in question.

"Didn't you ask her?" Rudy said with a frown.

Chagrined, Loch pressed his lips together before turning to the girl. "What's your name?"

The girl had been chewing on a bite of croquette. She stopped and slowly let it ooze from her mouth, down her chin and into her lap. Loch frowned. Aiden coughed. Rudy laughed.

"Maaaaaaaty," she drawled.

Loch glanced at Rudy and then Aiden. Rudy looked perplexed, Aiden shrugged.

"Matty?" Loch repeated.

"Maddy?" Aiden supplied.

"What?" Loch growled.

"Maddy," Rudy repeated. "*Madeline.*"

Aiden tensed before leaning forward and looking at the girl. "Dark hair, bright blue eyes," Aiden listed off. "You can't...you mean Madeleine *McGowan*?"

Loch pulled in a sharp breath. "The daughter of Ole Shirf?"

"*Great* grand-daughter, actually," Rudy said as he snuck the remaining hamburger half from the plate and took a bite while Loch and company were mildly stunned.

"That's a gutsy little far darrig," Loch's awed voice was foreign even to himself. "Shirfy isn't someone to be trifled with."

"*King* Shirfennelarfin to you," a small voice said from somewhere around Loch's knees.

He leaned down and watched the little pixie climb up a table leg and pull herself to the top, settling down next to Loch's plate with heavy breaths. The gargoyle regarded her physical state, a mangled wing, blue bruises on her face and silverish blood smudged on the side of her mouth. When she had somewhat recovered from her climb, she pointed at Loch and scowled.

"She's my hostage," the pixie sneered.

Loch couldn't help the chuckle that erupted from deep in his chest. "*Your* hostage?"

"This is *serious*," Aiden frowned as Loch noticed that Rudy had vanished, sometime between when the pixie had shown up and now.

Or maybe he could go invisible, Loch wondered. That gobshite had so many tricks up his sleeve that he wouldn't reveal, it was annoying to say the least.

"The only thing serious about this situation is that someone ate the rest of the burger I wanted to try and I ate *all* the cachopo."

Loch could feel the heat rising in Aiden's vicinity, and though the dragon had never *actually* set anything on fire by accident when he got mad, there was a first time for everything, so he grinned at his angry partner as he took one of the fabric napkins and scooped up the pixie. She screeched as he folded her gently inside and knotted the ends. He held up the now squirming bundle.

"We just need to get the pixie and the little girl back to HQ and we might be able to catch the end of the show."

Several puffs of smoke left the dragon's mouth as Loch placed the bundle onto the table and scooped up some potatoes.

"We are going to the authorities," Aiden stated.

"We *are* the authorities," Loch cocked his head and raised a brow at Aiden.

"We'll be the judge of that," a sweet accented voice said from behind them.

Chapter 5 - Aiden

Let's Step Outside And Have A Little Chat

Wednesday, 19 August 2015, 10:27 PM (El Boni restaurant in Spain)

"And who might you be?" Torloch asked, a touch defensively but with undeniable interest in the woman now standing at their table.

Her dark eyes and jet-black hair gave her a striking appearance, and her navy pantsuit uniform brought out the bronze highlights in her eyes. She flashed a badge, leaving the leather wallet open just long enough for Aiden to catch the *Guardianes de la Paz y la Orden de los Cronistas* - the Spanish

Keepers of the Peace and Order of Chroniclers - engraved in the metal.

"I am Officer-in-Training Emilia García, and this is my overseer Officer Mateo Fernández," she said with a brisk nod. "We are here to take you to Headquarters."

"A trainee?" Torloch said, his smile widening. "And what are we learning about today?"

Aiden fought the urge to groan and roll his eyes. Sometimes the gargoyle could pick the most *inconvenient* times to start flirting. This might be one of the worst.

"I have every power to enforce the laws and arrest you if necessary," she replied without missing a beat.

"Actually, we were just on our way out," Aiden said, his heart sinking as he thought about the international red tape and bureaucracy that they did *not* have time for right now. "We must return to Ireland immediately, it is a matter of-."

Officer Mateo Fernández stepped forward, putting up a meaty hand to stop the dragon's movement and explanation. The giant's shoulders were almost twice as wide as Aiden's, and he stood a full head above the dragon. His head was neatly shaved, and heavy brows pulled his face into a scary expression. He didn't speak, only gave a shake of his head and deepened his frown.

"-matter of grave importance," Aiden finished after a moment, unwilling to be pushed around.

"I'm sorry, but that won't be possible," the Officer-in-Training said, shoving the much larger man out of the way with a dirty look.

Marks were getting deducted for that, I'm sure, Aiden thought, noticing the giant's expression had somehow become even darker and scarier, and Torloch smirked as if he could hear the unspoken quip.

"And why is that?" Aiden asked.

"You cannot cross our borders through the Faeways and expect to have free reign about the country," she told him. "We'll need you to present proper identification, declare any items transported into the country, and your intentions regarding your stay."

"About that," Torloch jumped in smoothly. "We aren't intending to stay, and we haven't transported anything into the country that we won't be taking home with us when we go."

Maddy giggled happily, smashing a potato with a spoon on her plate. Aiden blinked. Her hair had turned to gold, and bright green eyes crinkled up at him when she beamed. She also looked considerably younger, closer to two years rather than three. *Rudy*, Aiden thought, and sent a prayer of thanks to the faery.

"This is your child?" Officer-in-Training Emilia asked.

"My sister's," Torloch said, without blinking. "Not that it's any of your business."

Emilia pursed her lips. "We have a VIP child-missing alert, so yes, it is our business when two foreign creatures come into the country illegally with a child."

VIP was a bit of an understatement in this case, Aiden thought, realizing they were about to be in much bigger trouble than he'd originally thought if they didn't get out of here.

Shirfennelarfin could best be described as a trust fund baby who had somehow managed to keep his shite together. He had inherited magic, wealth and an estate from his grandfather, Old Shirf, and lived in the same house the old man had inhabited. He was a very private man, and the most that was known about his business dealings were that they involved the purchase and transportation of fae art and artifacts.

The only reason Aiden knew anything about him at all was the fact that the King would fairly often deal with members of the Dragon Court, and either attempted to make a bid on an item already in a dragon's hoard, or provide his services to help acquire a particularly desired article. The first was borderline insulting per traditional dragon etiquette, but somehow he hadn't been flambéd, probably due to the second dealing, which was much appreciated by dragons as a whole.

Madeline cooed a bit, and Aiden looked back at her, disconcerted to find she looked like someone else, bright green eyes that were just a bit too emerald to be completely human.

"Does this look like the missing child?" Aiden asked, taking a leap of faith and hoping the glamor held for the two Officers.

Torloch kept his surprise under control when he glanced over and saw the change in the girl's aspect.

Emila pursed her lips as she examined the child for a long minute, and then looked at them sternly. "Still, you cannot come in unannounced."

"Like I said, we're just leaving," the gargoyle said, scooping up the child and jerking his head at Aiden.

Aiden quickly wet a napkin and cleaned Maddy as best he could, removing what looked like most of her dinner off her face and hands. He used the activity to get close enough to direct a tense whisper only Torloch could hear.

"Exactly how are we getting out of here, did you think?"

"Rudy," Torloch muttered in reply, his lips barely moving, bouncing the child gently so her happy gurgling concealed their conversation.

A cough caused them to turn and smile politely at the uniformed woman.

"Gentlemen, please don't cause a scene," she asked, her eyes more pleading than her tone. "If you are truly who you say, this won't take long at all."

The dragon and gargoyle looked at each other, both assessing the situation with ease. She needed this to go smoothly, to get her final marks, and leave the hulking brute at the academy so he could go and torture some other finishing student on their final practicals. Aiden took a moment to be impressed with the Spanish KPOC - he didn't recall specifically what he had needed to do to graduate, but it seemed a bit cruel and unusual to send an inexperienced student out to address a potential kidnapping over an international Faeways crossing.

Torloch pursed his lips, but took pity on her. "Alright, let's step outside and have a little chat. After I pay for the meal of course. It wouldn't do to be arrested by the Spanish constabulary."

She nodded at him gratefully, and the gargoyle artfully scooped up the napkin containing the criminally inclined pixie with his free hand, and put it in his pocket before they headed downstairs. As they walked, Aiden tried to find Rudy among the other patrons, but the sneaky prince had disappeared. *He better show up soon*, the dragon thought, clenching jaw. *He's our ticket out of here.*

The gargoyle paid for the meal, and moments later they emerged onto Rúa Portugal, a few pedestrians still out this late, but not near enough of a crowd to disappear into or be of any help whatsoever. The nondescript KPOC vehicle idled at the curb, a bored looking brownie in a chauffeur's hat sitting behind the wheel. A large black sedan with the Mercedes ornament waited across the street, looking very out of place in the empty street. Aiden frowned, and stopped walking. That was a bit weird.

The gargoyle had stopped too, with a strangled groan of pain as the child had grabbed his ear with all her might. Before he could do anything to help Torloch, the sedan shimmered away, revealing the glamored Faeway opening in a glimmer of moss and mud-colored sparkles, a goblin followed by several trolls piled out and started towards them. Aiden only had time to get a good look at the troll in front, noting the silver hoop in his ear, and the tattoos on his bicep, when a hand clutched the dragon's forearm, and he looked down to see the shimmering purple sparkles flying off Rudy. His other hand was attached to Torloch's coat hem.

"Hang on," the Unseelie prince warned, and the bright glow of a Faeways portal almost blinded the dragon.

He was pulled through the door, and along the insubstantial passageway at a dizzying speed. When solid ground was underneath his feet once more, he took a deep breath, the sweet smell of Irish air filling his lungs. He didn't think he had ever been so glad to be home. However...

"Rudy," he growled and opened his eyes. "What in Panthéa are you doing?"

"Saving your arses," Rudy said.

"Do you have any idea how many *additional* regulations we'll need to explain because of this?" Aiden said, throwing up his hands.

"Well, no," the faery admitted. "I *do* know they'll catch up eventually, probably, but hopefully we have enough time to get this sorted before then."

"So now we're on the run from the Spanish KPOC," the dragon spluttered. "That's just *great*, Rudy."

"Guys, trust me, you did *not* want to get in that car," the faery said, with emphatic hand gestures. "They would have taken the kid, and you would be stuck in Spanish gaol. And she-" he pointed an accusing finger at the bulge in the gargoyle's jacket where the pixie was safely stowed. "-*she* needs a *proper* introduction."

Chapter 6 - Loch
Where Has Your Delightful Bedside Manner Gone?

Wednesday, 19 August 2015, 11:02 PM (somewhere in Ireland...probably)

Loch was so happy to be away from the creepy giant (though he would have been glad to spend a little more time around the beautiful trainee) that he didn't give a rat's arse that Rudy had pulled them through the Faeway. He watched as the doorway they had just come through blinked out of existence, as Rudy and Aiden bickered about whatever they were bickering about.

The gargoyle could handle just about any inquiry thrown at him, whether it was from their Director or the Spanish KPOC, and felt quite confident that they would be found to be in the right. Pixie meddling or not. Speaking of...

"What do you mean a *proper* introduction?" he asked the sparkling faery, while juggling the squirming little girl in his arms and inspecting his environment.

They stood in a bright green meadow with a dusting of wild flowers and a light purple sky. A well worn path led through the meadow and a small cluster of trees. Just beyond there was a shimmer in the air as though what you saw wasn't true. Before Rudy could answer the question, Loch laughed.

"You brought us to the entrance of the Unseelie Court?" the gargoyle raised a brow.

Rudy shrugged. "Geez. It was the first place I thought of, okay? Shoot a guy for trying."

Aiden pressed his lips together, but a hint of laughter made his eyes crinkle. "Well perhaps we should find *another* place to discuss things? A place we won't stand out quite so much?"

Rudy's eyes bulged. "You guys are so picky. I *live* here. It's not *that* bad."

Loch placed a hand on Rudy's shoulders in a short lived endearment before the child tried to leap from his arms. He grabbed a better hold and she started to pout, a low whine starting somewhere in the base of her throat, and Loch was pretty sure they needed to let her down to stretch her legs very soon.

Eyes sparkling at a sudden thought, he looked at Aiden though he spoke to Roo. "Rudy, how about you take us to Claudine's home?"

Aiden let out a snort of steam and frowned at Loch. "Why would we go there?"

Loch smiled broadly. "Because no one would think to go there."

"Actually, they might. We do work together and she is probably better at dealing with a small child than we are," Aiden commented as he folded his arms across his chest and glared at Loch. "An even better idea is to go to Selena's house."

"Who's that?" Rudy scrunched his face in thought, "We don't want to involve just anyone. I don't know..."

"That's a terrible idea," Loch said. "She hates me."

"Exactly. No one would think to trace us there for that reason but also," Aiden smiled as he laid down his proverbial trump card. "Her family are well-known security experts."

The gargoyle couldn't tell if he was bluffing or not. "How did you know that?"

"I did a background check." The dragon looked at Loch with an almost insulted look, and the gargoyle gave a small shrug of apology. Of course Aiden had looked her up, and to be honest, wouldn't he have done the same? "They are the top recommended consultants for security and safeguarding, according to at least three dragons I asked."

Loch appreciated the dragon's thoroughness, but right now that was not helpful. "Dude, you're not getting it. She *really* doesn't want to see me."

"I have gathered something along those lines based on your ridiculous avoidance tactics at HQ, but this is the best solution we have right now. We can't stay in the Unseelie realm, not unless we want to turn this into a major diplomatic incident. We can't go home, and we can't go to HQ, not with KPOC Spain on our tail. The far darrig is out there somewhere. We don't have a lot of options."

Loch pressed his lips into a scowl, but the dragon had a compelling point he couldn't really argue with, which just made it all the more annoying.

"Fine," he said. "But this is probably not going to go well."

He rattled off the address. On the outside he didn't care one whit but on the inside, he could barely believe the nervous twitch in his stomach at the idea of seeing the vampire again, face to face and close enough to drown in the unique scent that only she possessed. Rudy sighed and shook his head as he grabbed each of them and pulled them through the Faeways once more. The doors passed by rapidly, and Loch had trouble keeping them apart as they blurred by.

"Are you sure you know where you're going?" he called up to the faery, keeping a death grip on Aiden's elbow with one hand, and Maddy with the other.

In answer, Rudy stopped at the next door, one which shifted and morphed into different shapes, all gothic and dreadful. The faery pushed it with all his might, but it held fast as he wrestled with the giant iron handle in the shape of a wolf and a raven entwined. Then it flew open wide, as if sucked by a great gust of wind, almost pulling the little faery off his feet as he exited the Faeways.

The others followed rapidly, and the Faeway entrance disappeared from around them with a pop, leaving them in darkness. Only faint starlight outlined vague shapes in silver. In the distance, an owl hooted, and was answered from across the way. Eyes blinking rapidly, Rudy squinted into the distance, and took a step forward. Immediately, motion-sensor lights flared to life, illuminating the short walls covered in ivy and the tree with boughs spreading overhead, the gates before them and the lawn beyond. A wide, pebbled drive bounded by a massive hedge led to a gray and black castle in the distance.

The faery turned to Loch. "She lives in a castle? By herself?"

Loch frowned. "Sort of. I mean it's not a true castle, but close enough. Selena's grandfather, well he's not really her grandfather but you know what I mean, he built it in the 1800's." He leaned down, and put his face very close to the faery's. "Now listen. Use your fake name, and keep your mouth shut as much as possible. Let's not blow your cover, right? You do not want to be on the bad side of Selena Windbourne, do you understand what I'm trying to say? This is *her domain*."

"Oooohhhhh, *thaaaaat* Selen*aaa*." Rudy managed to put a different sort of emphasis on each syllable that came out, in the most annoying way possible, and Loch's frown deepened, sure the faery was lying or pulling his leg.

Rudy puffed out his chest and tapped it impatiently. "Unseelie prince, hello?"

Just then, a tall, lean jet black dog with a tuft of blond hair between its ears lumbered around the castle across the front lawn, and stopped several feet away. It sat and watched them through the gate bars with intelligent golden eyes.

"Uh, guys, should we be worried about that?" Rudy's voice was a little higher than usual.

"Aww, look here," Loch said.

When Aiden and Rudy turned to him, he nodded his head at the sleeping child in his arms. "I guess she was tired."

"Yes, good. But the *dog*?" Aiden asked.

He wasn't concerned as animals tended to give dragons a wide berth, but Rudy looked ready to take flight.

Loch rolled his eyes. "No, it's just Lux."

At the gargoyle's words, the dog's tail wagged and it almost looked like he smiled.

"Hey, boy. Is your mam home?"

The dog dipped his head. Loch was glad but also disappointed. Looks like they were going to intrude, and there was no getting out of it.

Rudy cocked his head. "You know her dog?"

"I don't really but I keep tabs on things."

Aiden's lips quivered in a knowing smile and Loch turned away. Eh, he was fecked. A red light flashed and a beep sounded, then the gate opened, swinging outward without a sound.

"Looks like an invitation to me," Aiden said.

Yep, fecked.

They walked toward the front door, with Lux following behind them, trailing Rudy as the faery moved first to the left, then the right, trying to shift out of the dog's path. For a moment, a tickle of amusement eased the gargoyle's nervous butterflies, but as the front door loomed closer, not even Rudy's discomfort could banish the tight knot in his stomach.

Loch didn't know what would happen when Selena saw who was on her doorstep. Would she hiss and spit and tell him to feck off? Would she look right through him and pretend he didn't exist? Would she stab him? *Was it too late to back out?* The gargoyle looked around and saw they were almost at the door. Yes, it definitely was too late now. *I should come up with something to say*, he decided. *So I don't say the absolute wrong thing.*

Before Loch could come up with an interesting story for exactly why they were here at close to midnight on a Wednesday, the door opened and Selena stood there. The entire world descended into silence, only the thudding of his heart in his ears serving to remind Loch that time was still passing as he drank in the sight of the vampire. Bathed in the soft light from inside, she adjusted her frilly white robe with soft fuzzy stuff around the plunging neckline and cuffs.

"What are you wearing?" Loch asked and then immediately wanted to vanish in a poof of spectacular embarrassment. Especially because she looked wonderful, which may not have been precisely conveyed by his tone.

Selena narrowed her eyes and shook her head. "Where has your delightful bedside manner gone?"

Loch found himself. "Actually you look good enough to eat."

She grunted an acknowledgement as she gave him a judgmental once over before moving to look over everyone else with a cool gaze. She gave a nod to the dragon.

"Hello, Detective Moss."

Loch flinched at the small dismissal but he couldn't really blame his partner for her annoyance at Loch. He did deserve it after all, even if he didn't want to.

"Miss Windbourne," Aiden replied with a stately nod. "I'm sorry to inconvenience you at this hour."

The dragon had never seemed to fully grasp that vampires lived by slightly different rules and schedules than normal people did. Technically, it was her "morning", and when the sun rose in a few hours, it was traditionally her night, when she returned to bed or at least the protection of heavily tinted windows.

Ever gracious, Selena gave a wave. "It's no trouble. I slept in a little late so I've only just rolled out of bed."

Rudy pushed forward and gave a deep bow. "Miss Windbourne, allow me to introduce myself. I am Gavan Murphy, at your service."

The vampire looked down at the small faery with a momentary frown of confusion, which morphed into an expression of disinterest. "Yes, okay, thanks. Come inside and hang tight while I get dressed and then you can tell me what you're all doing here."

Rudy zipped in first, looking nervously over his shoulder at the dog following closely which Loch still thought was hilarious. Aiden went next, dipping his head at Selena as he passed. When Loch moved to step inside, Selena put a single finger against his shoulder, just below his clavicle, the light touch somehow enough to freeze him in place, sending electricity racing through him. The vampire spoke softly, to avoid waking Maddy. "I see you. I see the child. But why do I smell *pixie*?"

"Bullocks. I forgot about her."

A muffled response came from his pocket, the words jumbled, but the infuriated tone coming through as clear as day.

Selena sighed. "I don't want a pixie in my house. They are conniving little shites. Go around back. I'll bring everyone out in a minute and-" she looked back down at the sleeping child in his arms, and her face softened. "-I'll bring something for the little one."

"Thank you, Selena."

Her dark eyes moved up to his, and his heart went a little mushy. The vampire didn't say anything, just closed the door, leaving him to make his own way around to the back. His mind was buzzing, but completely and utterly blank as he tried to process what had just happened, and figure out if it was a good thing or likely to end up in future heartache for him.

He waited alone with his thoughts for less than two minutes on the luxurious back patio before Rudy and Aiden had joined him, and only a few more before Selena showed her face again. Now she wore a pair of black jeans and a black silk button up which left her pale arms bare. Her face was modestly done with eyeliner and a hint of powder, and her midnight black hair was pulled over her shoulder in an obsidian sheen. He blinked at her fast turnaround, then remembered vampiric speed.

She placed a royal-purple velvet cushion trimmed in black lace on the ground in between Aiden and Loch for the child and then sat on one of the comfortable outdoor rockers around a broad, round table. Lux lay down at her feet, blinking his great golden eyes

"All right, let's hear it."

Aiden filled her in as Loch grudgingly acknowledged that the dragon was best with the details of things, relaying the sequence of events in a complete fashion, without unnecessary added information. When he had brought her up to their untimely arrival on her doorstep, Loch turned to Rudy while pointing to the now squirming bulge in his jacket.

"Now, you said a *proper* introduction - what did you mean exactly?"

"Well..." the Unseelie prince paused. "Actually, I think you'd better let her out now. Hopefully it won't create a diplomatic incident."

Rudy was nodding up and down like a bobblehead as he spoke, and this was not filling Loch with a great sense of well-being. The gargoyle frowned as he placed the napkin on the table and unwrapped the pixie. She darted from the table and swooped around them all, a spluttering sparkle of pink, gold and green. As she let out some steam, Loch glanced at Aiden and suddenly felt the trouble he might have set himself up for. The look on the dragon's face could melt fire.

"For what it's worth," he commented to his friend. "I'm sorry in advance."

Aiden did not look impressed as the pixie landed on the table and glared first at Loch before turning on her heel and glaring at each person until she came full circle. She wore a sparkling clingy green gown with a jeweled tiara, an emerald centered on her forehead. Rudy took on a strange pompous arse-stature and bowed to the pixie.

"Madame Kynella Ghllyewyn," Rudy said with a courtly boom, then turned to introduce the others, motioning with a flourish to each person as he said their name. "Please meet Keepers of the Peace and Order of Chroniclers Detectives Aiden Moss and Torloch Doyle, and Vampiress Selena Windbourne of House Fletcher."

Loch raised a brow. Apparently the little fecker hadn't been lying. He watched Selena dip her head at the pixie, and then the regal gesture was returned in kind from Madame Kynella.

His chest gave a painful squeeze as he realized how much he had missed out on these past couple of centuries, since *The Incident*. The gargoyle was not in the habit of second-guessing himself, but he couldn't help but wonder how it could have been different. If someone else had been there with Selena's younger sister when she had died, then maybe, *just maybe*, Loch's young, newly-appointed-KPOC-detective self could have been the one to comfort Selena in her grief. Instead, they both drowned in the resulting mayhem and misunderstanding, which ended his newfound romance with Selena. His heart cracked a little bit more, and he shoved the memory and tangle of emotions away. *Not the time or place, Doyle,* he told himself sternly.

He brought his attention back to the present and the gathering on the outdoor patio to see the vampire shift gracefully and lift a hand to indicate another person behind them. "And right on time, may I present Green Witch Claudine Ní Mocháin."

Loch glanced up to see the petite young woman standing in the doorway. This evening she wore a pale sage-green bohemian skirt, with hand-embroidered flowers floating down the length, and a lavender cardigan that brought out the gray in her eyes. Dark hair was pulled back in a functional ponytail, and a chain of daisies woven through the green-streaked locks made her seem like the perfect subject for a Monet painting. When she saw everyone was looking at her, she tucked a strand of dark hair behind her ear and then waved shyly at everyone. "Selena called me when you guys arrived. She thought I might be able to help."

While Loch was almost completely riveted by the vampire, he managed to spare half a thought for his partner and glanced at Aiden. The dragon stood and bowed slightly at Claudine, in that stiff, standoffish way he had, which Loch absolutely *hated.* However, Claudine gave Aiden a sweet smile and sat down beside him. Not close enough to touch, but it was at least something. Loch was pleased with the slight progress, and he would have to talk to the dragon about it, because the dolt probably hadn't noticed.

"Help with what?" Rudy asked.

"Whatever trouble you have gotten yourself into this time, is what I told her," Selena said without apology. "Apparently a kidnapping, which Madame Kynella can shed some further light on, if I'm not mistaken."

"It's not a *kidnapping*, I merely borrowed the child," the pixie sneered at everyone again and let her gaze fall on the vampire. "And for the record, I am *not* a conniving little shite."

Selena simply looked at her and bent her head to the side. "Prove it."

"Ah guys," Rudy started in. "Madame Kynella Ghllyewyn is one of three high priestess of the pixie kinfolk of the Stoney-matter county mound."

He looked around, as if this gave some clue as to what they should do next, but Loch thought that maybe Rudy was giving the little creature a bit more pomp and circumstance than she really deserved. The pixie had admitted to taking the child for the ransom. What more evidence does one need to just take her into KPOC for questioning?

Honestly, the little girl's Da might be wondering where his offspring was as well. He started to wonder if Selena had any food in her house as he glanced at the little girl, Maddy, to see how she was faring. Tucked in a circle around her teddy bear, she slept soundly.

"Madam Kynella, if I may inquire," Aiden stated, with perfect courtly manners. "What is the reason you have for *borrowing* this particular child?"

Finally an interesting question, Loch would high five his partner if he wasn't sure it would get him burned.

The pixie opened her mouth to reply, but at that moment, Rudy leapt up as if he had been bitten.

"Guys...incoming!" the faery yelled before launching himself under the table and vanishing in a puff of purple sparkles.

Chapter 7 - Aiden
Your Wish Is My Command

Thursday, 20 August 2015, 12:02 A.M. (Residence of Selena Windbourne)

As the purple sparkles faded, teal and silver sparkles sprung into being, swirling like a whirling dervish. Torloch yelled something that could have been an old Gaelic war cry, but Aiden was a little preoccupied with the nature of the mystery guests. He stood and moved in front of the sleeping child, ready to protect her from whatever came through the fae ways portal materializing in front of him. He wasn't quite sure how kindly a vampire would take to a full-grown dragon destroying her back patio, but he supposed he could worry about that later.

"Everyone, please remain calm," Madame Kynella Ghllyewyn said, pitching her tiny voice loud, holding her minute hands out. "It's only my handmaidens."

As her voice described, two figures matching her stature appeared, wearing similar garb and tiaras, though their emeralds were much smaller, only tiny chips in the wrought metal, and their dresses were not quite as vibrant or sparkly as the high priestess's. The sparkles faded after a moment, returning the lighting to only the soft glow of outdoor night-lights.

"How exactly did you get into my house?" Selena asked before anyone could move, her voice dangerously soft.

Kynella waved her hand, and then staggered a bit, sitting down heavily and propping herself into a sitting position against a flowerpot. "I assisted them through your wards."

"And this is supposed to convince me that you're *not* a conniving little shite? This is why I don't let pixies in my house!" Selena fumed, but once she heard the explanation, she seemed to calm down

Also, seeing the conniving pixie in question severely winded and depleted of energy after using her magic probably helped reinforce the vampire's trust in the strength of her wards.

"Madame!" the first handmaiden cried, her tiny hand going to her mouth, her eyes wide and horrified as she beheld her high priestess's bruised face and crumpled left wing. "Who did this to you?"

"That would be the large one with the pretty face," Kynella said, waving at Torloch.

All eyes turned to the gargoyle, whose chagrin morphed into something resembling nervousness when he beheld their fury. Aiden found this a bit funny, seeming as the three pixies were about the size of the gargoyle's thumb, but he knew what the curses of the little people could do, and you did *not* want to incur their wrath.

"Yes, the gargoyle did this, but it was in service of protection of a child, so he is forgiven," Kynella said after a moment of watching Torloch squirm.

The tension eased palpably, and Aiden breathed a sigh of relief. That could have gotten uglier than he wanted to think about. He noticed Claudine put something back in her pocket, and Selena's fists slowly unclenched. *She really did not like pixies, that one.*

"Okay," the dragon announced loudly, remembering his original question. "Let's get to the bottom of this, shall we? What is your business with this child?"

The little pixie sighed, and rubbed the bridge of her nose. "I never meant to hurt her, I swear to you. King Shirfennelarfin has something that belongs to me, and I want it back."

"So you kidnapped his daughter?" Torloch asked, incredulous. "That doesn't sound very intelligent." Kynella Ghllyewyn glared at him, and he put his hands up. "I mean, couldn't you just send him some chests of gold or jewels, or something?"

"What use would a person like Shirfennelarfin have for gold, and fae gold at that?" the pixie said. "No, this was the only way."

Aiden snorted, a trail of smoke curling up to illustrate his disbelief. "You could have gone to the Five Courts," he said. "That was another option."

"You think I haven't tried that?" Kynella threw her hands up.

"Okay, okay," Aiden said. "What is it that he's got that you want?"

"A candle," the pixie said.

"This is not just any old candle?" Selena piped up.

"No, it belonged to Oisín," Kynella said, a careful measure to her tone.

"Oisín...of the Fianna?" Aiden said.

"No, Oisín who works at the eatery on Montague Street," Kynella replied dryly. "Yes, Oisín of the Fianna. He brought it back from Tír na nÓg. Well, he brought back three, but this is the one I need returned to me."

"So you're telling me that Shirfy has this candle...and you think it belongs to you, for some reason you haven't fully explained?" Torloch asked.

"He can keep the candle," Kynella said. "I only want what it contains."

An expectant silence fell over the room, and the priestess crossed her arms, setting her face in an obstinate pout.

"You're not going to tell us?" Selena said, managing to look offended, surprised, unimpressed, and inquisitive all at the same time.

"It's a private matter," the pixie replied pertly.

"It's a candle," the gargoyle said. "How private can it be?"

"Not very bright, the pretty one is," the second handmaiden said, and the first snickered.

"I'll squash you too, don't think I won't," Torloch warned them.

Aiden put a hand up. "Alright, alright, simmer down."

"You simmer down," Torloch retorted. "They're not insulting *your* intelligence."

"Why is the candle important?" Claudine asked, the sensible witch deftly turning the conversation back to the matter at hand.

Madame Kynella Ghllyewyn looked at her, and something about the young witch's kind eyes and attentive expression extinguished the irate fire simmering in the pixie.

"The candle contains a wish." Kynella looked sad. "It was placed there by my grandmother, before she died. I just want to get the wish back."

"And...what did the far darrig do to get involved?" Torloch said, his eyes narrowed as he put all the pieces together, finding them not quite fitting as nicely as they should.

"I needed some help getting the girl away," she said. "He owed me. She glared at the people gathered around her. "And currently he still owes, based on his *miserable* performance."

"Well now, that's a bit harsh," Aiden said. "We're actually quite-"

"No, I'd say that was fair,' Torloch butted in, unhelpfully. "His kidnapping was horribly botched, you have to admit."

"I was *going to* point out we're *actually* quite good at what we do," Aiden said stiffly. "So it wasn't just incompetence on his part."

"Right," the gargoyle nodded. "That's fair too."

"It was supposed to be quiet," the priestess lamented. "No one else was supposed to know, or be involved, *especially* not the KPOC."

"How did the girl escape from him?" Selena asked. "From my experience with the Red Caped, that is hard to believe."

Kynella cursed softly. "You can thank that daft amadan Ruaidhr-"

Aiden coughed violently, and Torloch looked up with a bright expression.

"You mean Garvan?" the gargoyle asked in a bright tone.

The priestess looked like she wanted to contradict him, but she composed herself and nodded. "Of course. Garvan."

Rudy may have been annoying - and presently *suspiciously* absent - but he was still *prince* Ruaidhrí mac ríona, son of Queen Mab of the Unseelie Court. Whatever quarrel the high priestess had with him would be expressed in layers of polite discourtesy, and solved with expensive tokens and flowery platitudes of remorse, *out* of the public eye.

"The idiot distracted my far darrig, and the girl slipped away."

"Clever girl," Torloch said, with a proud smile.

"Clever Rudy," Aiden said, and the gargoyle shrugged in agreement.

"What we need is a plan," Selena said. "Some way to get to Shirfennelarfin with his daughter *annnnd-*" she drew the word out with a glare at the pixie to shut her up even as her mouth opened to protest, "-get Madame Kynella her candle, to retrieve her wish."

"I thought you didn't like pixies," Torloch said.

"I don't," the vampire replied, batting her eyelashes at him twice. "But if it belongs to her, she has a right to have it."

"Does anyone know how to get into Shirfennelarfin's domain?" Aiden said. "I mean, it's not like we can just walk in."

"I have an idea," Claudine spoke up, and all eyes turned to her. "That could work, I think, although it might be a bit complicated. What if we-"

A shrill alarm sounded and all eyes went to Selena as she pulled out her phone.

"We have more visitors," the vampire said, and turned the device to show them the surveillance feed from her front door camera.

Three figures stood at the step, and Aiden recognized one of the trolls from the restaurant, the one with the earring and the tattoos on his arm. The other two he did not know, and had the strong feeling that he did not *want* to know them.

"What's the plan?" Torloch demanded, rounding on Claudine.

"They want the girl," the witch said, no longer mincing her words. "What if we give her to them?"

"That's a *terrible* idea," the gargoyle said.

"Not the *real* girl," Claudine said. "A copy. Something that *looks* like her."

"A changeling," Aiden said, catching on to her idea, and she nodded.

"Exactly."

"That's a brilliant idea," the gargoyle said. "And we have just the people we need to pull that off."

He smiled at the two handmaidens, standing protectively by Kynella, and they glared up at him. The high priestess sighed.

"I'll just need a moment," she said, waving at the other two pixies who came closer immediately, though they both had reluctant expressions.

"They've gone around to the side," Selena said softly, eyes glancing down at the security footage flashing across her phone. "Lux will head them off, but that won't keep them forever."

"Feck," Aiden cursed. "Are you ready?"

"Almost," the priestess said, then turned and gestured behind her.

Three identical Maddies slept side-by-side, clutching three identical teddy bears.

"Which one is her?" Torloch asked with a frown.

"You can't tell?" Kynella said, her eyes lighting up.

"That one is Maddy," Claudine said, gesturing at the one in the middle. "I was keeping an eye on her."

Kynella's face fell, but she nodded. Torloch scooped up the real girl, who simply snuggled into his arms and continued sleeping. Claudine took one of the others, and Selena set the last one on her seat, and arranged blankets around her, to conceal her.

"Go," she waved at Torloch. "I'll distract them for as long as I can."

"Madame Kynella, you're with us," Aiden said. "We are going to do this *our* way, none of your shenanigans."

"Naturally," the pixie said with a resigned sigh. "Where to from here?

"Headquarters," the dragon said firmly.

"Of the KPOC?" Kynella asked, raising her brow.

"No, of Butler's Chocolates," Aiden said, mimicking her earlier tone. "Yes, of the KPOC."

"And here I thought you were the brains of this outfit," the high priestess said. "You can't just portal someone into KPOC Headquarters through the wards, are you mad? Besides, if the KPOC gets wind of this scheme, they'll take the child right out of *your* hands, and then where will we be?"

"Right," Aiden said, knowing he should have thought of that.

"What about the eatery on Montague street?" Torloch suggested with an evil grin. "The one Oisín works at?"

"That wouldn't be open at..." Aiden tried to say, but the pull of the Faeways was already moving them into the misty corridors.

"Your wish is my command," the voice of the pixie followed them as Selena's house disappeared.

Chapter 8 - Selena
What Do You Want with the Little Human?

Thursday, 20 August 2015, 1:13 A.M. (Residence of Selena Windbourne)

Selena was stunned when Torloch Doyle, of all people, showed up on her doorstep out of the blue, holding a child no less.

She had kept her composure, but now his rapid exit via the Faeways made her wonder if she was having a dream. She had yet to decide if it was a good dream or a bad dream - one half of her heart rushing forward, the other half running away. A wave of relief had overwhelmed her when she realized the child belonged to someone else - not Loch - and she'd been frozen in shock for a moment, but she was glad he hadn't noticed.

The vampire was saved from having to make any decisions of the heart by Claudine tugging on her arm, pointing at the shadows moving across the screen.

"Hide!" Selena hissed to the green witch, who was cradling one of the fake Maddies in a very maternal way.

The vampire waved a hand at a large potted plant behind her and a large shrub with branches entwined densely to her left. Claudine ducked under the branches, and helped Selena set them just so, to hide her completely. With no time to spare, Selena sat on a lounge chair, her legs stretched before her, feet crossed at the ankle. She unbuttoned the top two buttons on her black, silk shirt and held her phone to her ear.

"Can you believe it?" she said to no one. "Talk about a couple of incompetent-"

The three thugs rounded the corner of the house and spotted her. Lux growled and if one watched carefully, they might have noticed his size slowly increase.

"It's okay, boy. I am very sure these gentlemen must be lost." Selena stood up, pocketed her phone and rested her hands on her hips. "Can I help you gentlemen?"

"Where's the child?" the smaller of three trolls asked.

Even the smallest was a foot taller than the vampire, but it was no matter. What she lacked in size, she made up for in spades with brains *and* speed. She noticed a fourth intruder, skulking several feet behind them. Dark skinned with random tufts of brown fur and large, bulbous eyes, the goblin watched with a bored expression.

Still, Selena was unconcerned. She'd like to see them try anything. She may not be hungry right *now*, but she could easily take down at least one and if she was honest with herself, they were a very tasty treat, and it wouldn't be much of an inconvenience.

"What do you want with the little human?" the vampire asked, crossing her arms.

"*Magic* human," one of the other trolls commented, earning him a back hand from the little one.

Sometimes it really is the small ones that you need to look out for. She was reminded of pixies but refrained from scowling.

"Sorry, Frah," the big troll said in a sulky tone, rubbing his jaw.

The smaller rolled his eyes and scowled.

"Well? What do you want with her?" Selena grilled.

"None of your business," Frah answered.

"Oh, I think it is," Selena showed her teeth in an unfriendly smile.

"She must be returned to her rightful owner."

"*Owner*? Really?"

The tallest and scariest looking of the trolls with fists the size of her head coughed into one of his meaty hands, concealing some merriment at her comment. Glad she could entertain someone.

"Her father," the littlest troll corrected.

"And how do I know you're not just going to make off with her and collect the ransom yourself?" she asked.

The troll groaned. "Come on lady. You can trust us."

Now Selena refrained from laughing. "Well, if that's what you're doing, go ahead and take her," the vampire motioned to the bundle of blankets on the sofa chair she had vacated earlier. "What the heck am I going to do with a human child? Can't eat them, can't train them..." She trailed off and shrugged as if they might understand her woes.

All three trolls watched her skeptically. Selena rolled her eyes and walked over. She nudged the blanket to the side so they could see the wee girl sleeping peacefully. The trolls moved closer and it was then that Selena realized her mistake, just a bit too late.

The oversized bald troll threw out a fist and caught her smack in the face. Flying back, Selena hit the ground with a thud, her nose and lip throbbing. She reached up and snapped her nose back into place as she felt blood flow down her cheek, the salty flavor filling her mouth.

"You dumb fecks," Selena hissed before she let out a low laugh. "He will catch you, and then you'll wish you were never born."

Which was true, *if* the child was real - the gargoyle wouldn't give two fecks about them, but they didn't know that.

The medium sized troll laughed. "Not likely. First he'd have to get through the King's newly enforced alarms and second, they'd have to get through us."

"Who is he?" Frah asked, his eyes narrowed.

Selena gave him a rude gesture.

The other troll chuckled some more. "Seriously, Frah, there's no way anyone could get through the pressure steps and no one in their right mind would attempt the steaming pit of dunnel frogs. It's a death call."

Frah raised his eyes to the sky and glared at the troll. "You dumb arse. Shut your mouth!"

The troll shrugged. "Just trying to be helpful."

"Well, stop trying to be helpful, and just do what I tell you!"

Selenea watched as the middle troll scooped up the bundle of blanket, glad that the child inside wasn't actually real. The troll then turned to the goblin who had moved close to them. The goblin held out its arms, and each troll latched on and then vanished in a flash of light into a Faeway. Trolls couldn't move through the Faeway by themselves, thus the goblin.

Selena moved to stand, wincing, as Claudine burst from her hiding spot and rushed over.

"Oh, my goodness, Selena, are you alright?"

"Of course, I'll be fine. Head still attached and all that, nothing harmed except my pride. I'm glad Lo-" she cut herself short and gave Claudine the side-eye. "I wouldn't have wanted anyone to see that."

Claudine smiled in understanding and placed a hand on Selena's arm. "*He* will not be pleased, I think."

Selena ignored the comment and focused on the pain as her nose healed. Staring at the place where the trolls had vanished, she turned her head to the place where Loch had vanished from her sight, imagining he was still standing there.

Despite the fact that the big oaf had brought this to *her* house of all places, she still had a tinge of worry in her belly. The gargoyle wouldn't take much care to be safe, she knew that. It was unsettling to care so much after so many years and after what he had done-

Despite attempting to calm her heart when Loch was near, it defied her at every turn and swelled in joy when she saw him. Sometimes she wanted to give in and forget the fact that he had-

Selena stopped herself from going down that path. What was broken, was done. There was nothing her heart could do to change the past. Claudine held the still sleeping bundle in her arms. She looked at the child and smiled as she adjusted the blanket.

"She's so real," she commented.

Selena raised a brow. "Ever think you'll have children?"

Claudine blinked before looking at her friend, and wrinkling her nose in a hopeful yet not entirely committal expression. "I hope to, some day."

"Good. I want to be the politically incorrect auntie." The vampire bared her fangs in a smile.

Claudine rolled her eyes but her smile showed she enjoyed the thought of it.

"Apparently, the child will hold that form for a couple hours at least. The magic isn't exact," Selena shared.

"Hopefully the boys are making some headway. Selena, mind if I borrow a car? I'm going to take this one to Headquarters, as I think that will be safer." The witch chewed her lip a little nervously. "Those henchmen will show up again, I'm sure."

Selena smiled at her friend. "Of course. Take the SUV in the garage. I'm going to find the guys to see what I can do to help."

"Oh, really, you want to help the KPOC with a case? Wouldn't have anything to do with a tall strapping gargoyle?"

Selena scowled at the witch. "I'll have you know that I've been on contract with the KPOC for longer than you've been alive. So, most definitely *not*. Now get off with you. I'll be in touch with any updates."

A barely audible pop made Selena crouch, getting ready to attack. The shining smile of Rudy floated bodiless for a moment before the rest of him appeared and settled on the grass before her.

"Hey, what did I miss?"

"Ah, excellent timing, faery."

The faery in question looked very nervous at her enthusiastic greeting, but that just made Selena smile more.

Chapter 9 - Loch
The Feck

Thursday, 20 August 2015, 1:02 A.M. (Dublin)

Even knowing she could protect herself, Loch did not like leaving Selena - or Claudine, for that matter - behind with the decoy while he and Aiden took the easier route with the kid. With a gargoyle's innate instinct for protection, the whole thing felt wrong to him on so many levels. The moment the portal spat them out inside the delicious toastie shop on Montague street, he felt a little more grounded. With the prospect of food in his future, he smiled. *Everything was going to be okay.*

Aiden frowned and a curl of smoke left his nose. "As I was *trying* to explain earlier, there's no one *here* at this time of the *day*. Or night. And Kynella, why on earth did you put us *inside* the bloody place? How are we going to get out?"

Loch raised a brow, the dragon must be pretty irritated to forget his manners and address the high priestess in *that* tone - the one he usually reserved for lecturing the gargoyle. He then checked on Maddy, confirming that she was still sleeping and looked around the restaurant. The dragon was of course correct. At one o'clock in the morning, everything was still, quiet, and dark, the navy walls made the place seem even darker. Chairs and tables were just blurs, a faint nightlight glinted off the lights hanging over the back counter, and the ovens and glass serving trays were empty, though the promise of melted cheese and butter-toasted bread lingered. His lips started to turn down in frustration but then his eyes brightened.

"Not a problem! I know just the thing!"

He went to the front door, unlocked it, and pulled it open. An alarm shouted from above, an answering startled wail sounded from Loch's arms.

"You eejit," Aiden muttered as he shoved out the door behind Loch and closed it quickly behind him.

The alarm continued to berate them.

"Kynella, can you go lock the door and meet us back here?" Loch asked surprisingly nicely. "Oh, and crash their video, would you?"

He grimaced as the pixie rolled her eyes and flashed out of sight. "I'll send them a bank draft for the false alarm fee. I just don't want them to think someone broke in."

"Someone *did* break in," Aiden grumbled as they quickly made their way down the well-lit street.

"Yes but technically we didn't *break* in, and it was an accident *and* we didn't steal anything, so it doesn't count," the gargoyle said, though he knew none of those very good reasons would appease Aiden when he had his mind set on being in a grumpy mood. It wouldn't appease Warren, the KPOC's leprechaun leader, no matter his mood.

Loch stopped several buildings down and knocked three times on an unassuming green door, then leaned close to the weathered wood.

"Luck is Bullocks," he stated.

Only a few seconds passed and then the door opened wide.

"Bullocks I tell ya!" bellowed the little man before them.

He just came up to Loch's elbow and had a wild orange beard and equally alarming hair, partially tucked beneath a green top hat. He wore green tracksuit bottoms and a dark green sweater with lime stripes. A hammer was hung on a rope around his waist and yet he wore no shoes.

Maddy started to sniff and fuss in Loch's arms. He turned to Aiden and shoved the squirming bundle into the dragon's care before turning back to the leprechaun and giving him a hug, lifting him off his bare feet and setting him down again.

"Aye, Raffie, you whining shite, how are ye?" Loch queried as he released the man in question.

"I'm well, Torloch Conall of the clan Dubhghaill," Raffie waved them inside and closed the door. "What brings your sorry arse to my shop? Are ye lost?"

The shop smelled of cinnamon and leather. On the longest wall to their left was shelf after shelf filled with hand tailored shoes and boots of all colors, shapes and sizes. On their right was a large case filled with a pile of assorted home-baked cookies, and an espresso machine sat on a counter next to a large fridge.

Loch chuckled at his old friend. "Actually, I was hoping for a favor. I need a place for us to hang out for a few hours, maybe twist your miserly hand for a bite or two and then we're out of your hair. We have an evil plan to concoct and need a safe place to do so."

The leprechaun grinned.

"Well, lad, you've come to the right place. I was just tellin' the missus what a bore things were."

He glanced over the four of them - Loch, who needed a clothing change and had been lugging around a child still covered with mud from her playdate with the pixie and a significant portion of a Spanish dinner; Aiden who was somehow close to immaculate and now held said child who had one droopy eye opened and leveled at the leprechaun and finally the scowling pixie who had alighted on a leather chair near the front door.

Loch frowned. She'd been surprisingly quiet.

The leprechaun dipped his chin at the pixie. "Madame Kynella."

"Sir Raffarn Viridi Silva," the pixie replied.

Aiden raised a brow, and looked at Loch's old friend with new interest. "Knight of the Green Forest?"

"Hush," the little man said with a wave. "That was a long time ago. Come upstairs. The babe can sleep a wink while ye work. I've still three pair to finish and deliver by morning. You'll have to excuse me from the party, I'm busy." He looked at Loch and his face softened. "Don't ye worry, I'll send the ball and chain up with snacks shortly."

Loch smiled. "Many thanks."

They followed Raffie up a flight of narrow, hollow stairs, turned and then went up another flight. He pointed at two doors, one bright yellow, the other green, before turning and heading back down the stairs.

Aiden held the girl, bobbing her gently as he stared at nothing. They had been up for quite a while, and strong coffee was definitely in order. First, a place to put the child. Loch opened the first door and saw a double bed, he waved Aiden inside.

The dragon walked over and placed the little girl on one of the beds. She must have been very tired as she gripped her bear closer and rolled over, and let out a soft sigh while Aiden pulled the covers around her.

After closing the door gently, they headed to the next door but hadn't even gotten it open before a thin wail erupted from the room that had just left. They looked at each other, a silent face-off with the loser being the one who would have to deal with the little one this time.

"Oh, what have we got 'ere?" a high pitched voice came from the steps behind them.

Loch turned and smiled at Mrs. Silva. A short leprechaun with a pointy nose, mostly white hair piled on top of her head, only a hint of red in the curls, wearing a plaid apron over a gray dress arrived at the top of the stairs, a large tray laden with cheese, meat, sliced bread, a clump of butter and cookies in one hand. And, as if she had read his mind, a steaming french press of coffee was in the other. Loch bowed.

"A sight for sore eyes, Mrs. Silva."

She giggled. "Oh, you rascal. Let me through."

Aiden had opened the door to the second room for her, and she whisked by him and put the trays down on a round table. The others filed in behind her. The room was decked out in a kaleidoscope of colors, and the sofas and comfy chairs were all covered in blankets or throws, knitted or crocheted in every color of the rainbow. From a drawer in the sideboard, Mrs. Silva pulled out small plates and mugs, and presented them to her guests. She flourished her hand at the food on the table with a warm smile.

"Eat boys, I will take care of the wee one."

"You are a saver of all that is life," Loch spouted. "And more gorgeous each time I lay eyes on you."

She patted him on the arm as she passed. "Suck up."

He watched her go out the door and close it behind her. A moment later, the wailing, which had ramped up to high volume crying, quieted. The dragon and gargoyle both sighed and slumped into the comfortable old chairs at the table. The pixie sat on the edge of one of the plates and with a miniscule dagger she'd pulled out of somewhere, broke off a piece of a chocolate chip cookie.

Aiden poured himself a cup of coffee, and found the jug of cream nestled in the middle of the bread and cookies. He took a gulp and sighed in appreciation before picking up a slice of bread and slathering it with butter and a heaping of cheese and ham. "I don't think we should stay here too long. Those thugs are bound to be here shortly. They must have some sort of tracking or locating spell on the child."

"She did," Kynella said. "But I've shielded it."

Loch shrugged. "So the girl's safe, it's not a big deal if we're not in any hurry."

"Wrong," came the tinny voice of the pixie. "Cherun is in danger, my handmaiden is in the clutches of those trolls, and the King has set up more wards and guards, with trolls and now ogres and werewolves walking his land. It's like trying to break into the Unseelie lands!"

"Don't be so dramatic," Loch said, thinking of all the secure places they'd gotten in and out of, some less gracefully than others, but still.

The pixie sighed.

"Oh *shite*!" The dragon's face scrunched up into an expression of agony.

"What?" Loch said, immediately looking around the room for danger, an impending attack of a rabid werewolf or something of the sort.

"I wanted to get the pork chops brining overnight," Aiden said, staring at his watch as somehow, magically, that would make it possible to still do that.

"A," Loch said as patiently as he could. "We kind of have bigger problems at the moment."

"Until we *don't*, and then you'll be winging about 'where is dinner?'," Aiden muttered, apparently very put out.

The gargoyle rolled his eyes. He wasn't *that* whiny, even when hungry. "So what is our plan?"

"I've been thinking about that," the dragon said slowly, the dinner fiasco quickly forgotten. "What if we-"

The door to the room swung open and Selena strolled in, with Rudy on her heels. Raffie was right behind them, glaring at the vampire, who had apparently just strolled in without much of an invitation, judging by the leprechaun's look.

"She said she was a friend of yours," he said by way of explanation for the unannounced intrusion.

"I said they were *expecting* me," Selena said.

Loch noticed immediately that she had changed clothing, and now wore a more practical, kick-butt outfit - leather pants, boots, a t-shirt and jacket. He eyed the light bruising around her nose, and an angry fire sparked in his chest, starting his blood boiling. For a vampire to have such marks meant some serious damage had been done not too long ago. He strode over to her.

"What happened to you?" he demanded.

Though she was several inches shorter than he was, she still managed to look down her not-quite-healed nose at him. "If you must know," she said stiffly, "I had a run in with a troll but I'm fine. This will be fully healed shortly."

She attempted to wave him off but he wouldn't budge.

"Which one?" he asked with quiet intensity.

She shrugged, and seemed to realize he wasn't going to let it go without an answer. "The bald idiot with hands the size of dinner plates, the feck."

Loch felt hot steam build in his shoulders. The thought of anyone hurting Selena just-

She shoved him out of the way, and slid into the chair he had vacated, selecting a cookie from the tray with confidence.

"Help yourself," Aiden said in a bemused tone, and she gave him a sardonic smile.

"Funny, I don't remember you being so particular when *you* crashed *my* place without asking," she said.

"You have a point there," the dragon allowed with a nod.

"How did you find us?" Madame Kynella asked, her face leery.

The vampire smiled. "Garvan *may* have helped."

The pixie narrowed her eyes at the faery prince, who put on his best innocent face, and looked at anything in the room but her.

"And what are you doing here?" she asked. "You're supposed to be a decoy."

"I was, and now I'm not. I did get some updated intel on the security," Selena said, and delicately brushed a crumb from the corner of her mouth. "You'll need it for whatever plan you hatch."

The pixie did not look very happy, but nodded before turning back to Aiden, hands on her hips. "You were saying?"

Aiden drummed his fingers on the table. "I have an idea. Maybe...maybe we're thinking about this too hard, making it too complicated."

"When have we ever made something too complicated?" Loch asked, mostly to annoy him, but a little bit because he was interested in the specific events the dragon would choose to illustrate the point.

Aiden ignored him. "What if we just returned Maddy to her father, give her back without any further ado?"

Chapter 10 - Aiden
We Need A Car

Thursday, 20 August 2015, 2:15 A.M. (Dublin)

"So, just to make sure I understand this - you think it's a *good* idea to bring her right to Shirfennelarfin?" Madame Kynella said, and looked at Torloch. "He does realize that defeats the entire point of my plan to get the wish back, right?"

"No, it doesn't," Aiden explained patiently. "You admitted yourself that there is no way you can get into his estate. We *can*. And once we're on the inside..."

The pixies eyes slowly brightened, and a smile twitched at the corner of her mouth. "So, you get in, and then?"

"We can get you in through the wards without being detected, at least right away," the dragon said.

"And just how do you think we'll be able to do that?" Torloch asked with a frown. "Last I checked, we don't know the exact layout and design of any of his security features."

"You're right," Aiden said with a smile. "But *she* does."

He nodded at Selena, who was draped in the comfy chair, examining her silver-tipped, black painted nails as if they were the most fascinating thing in the world.

"My family may have helped his grandfather design the defenses for his estate," the vampire shrugged.

Torloch's eyebrows nearly flew off his face, but then he managed to get a handle on his surprise.

"Well, that's nice for him, I suppose," the gargoyle said.

"It is," Selena grinned. "They're practically impervious."

"Practically?" Torloch said.

"You didn't think a vampire would design a *perfectly* impenetrable defense, with no back door whatsoever?" Selena raised a brow. "We live for a very long time. It is impractical to assume that the current circumstances will last forever, and we are *very* good at making sure things always go our way, no matter who is in or out of favor."

"I know that," Torloch said. "I also know he's had a *very long* time to poke around and discover the little cracks you built in."

"You don't really *live* for a very long time," Aiden said, the choice of words bugging him.

"That's very true," Selena told Torloch, both the vampire and the gargoyle ignoring the dragon. "And believe it or not, I am taking that into consideration. Shirfennelarfin hasn't tripped *all* the warning wards in place, so I should be able to provide a safe route for you and the pixie."

"What I want to know," Aiden said. "Is how a *human* circumvented Five Courts law to receive athanasia from the fae? I'm pretty sure there are *a lot* of ordinances against that particular gift being bestowed on..."

"Not athanasia, just very long life," Kyynella clarified with an affronted glare. "He's not *immortal*. He will die. Eventually."

She sounded as though that day was too far off for her liking, even though she would outlive him by centuries.

"Well," Selena made sure to show some extra teeth in her smile. "It was before the Five Courts were allies and the Codex brought into being. And the rest is a tale for another time. You'll need a car."

"Why?" Torloch crossed his arms, then uncrossed them.

"Unless you want to be shot out of the sky, you'll have to go through the main gate, declare yourself like a normal person, and be escorted up the drive and through the front door," Selena said.

The gargoyle did not look happy about the idea that *anything* could shoot him out of the sky, but the vampire did know him rather well, and was familiar with his abilities. If she said Shirfennelarfin's security was that good, it was probably that good.

"Where do we get a car?" Aiden said, thinking about how far the garage at home was.

"Oi, Raffy!" Loch cupped a hand around his mouth and yelled in the general direction of the first floor and the leprechaun's workshop.

A muffled thud, some scuffling, then the light footsteps of the leprechaun came towards them.

"You called, my lord?" Sir Raffarn said from the doorway with a heavy sigh and an eye roll, a half-finished shoe in one hand, a small silver hammer in the other.

"We need a car."

"I suppose you can borrow mine," Raffarn said.

"Good man," Torloch beamed.

They followed Raffarn outside, and he waved at his vehicle. Aiden and Torloch looked at it for a long moment. The gargoyle leaned closer and spoke in a low voice.

"Do you think we'll fit?"

"We most certainly will not fit," Aiden replied, looking at the green two-door mini cooper, that might as well have been a slipper for all the good it was going to do them.

"Right," Torloch said with a nod. "Plan B?"

"You could go get one of yours," Aiden told him. "You did want to fly, remember?"

The gargoyle gave him a dirty look, then pulled off his shirt. "I'll be back in a jiffy."

Aiden tried very hard not to notice the vampire's eyes light up in appreciation of the unveiled view, but it was a wee bit difficult as it was obvious she was enjoying it immensely. They all watched Torloch launch himself into the sky, and stood around the deserted pavement for a moment longer before returning to the room to wait.

Aiden had another cup of coffee, and a biscuit, wondering if his plan was going to work. Now that he had some time alone with his thoughts, he was second guessing it. He rubbed his hands as he thought. He didn't know what kind of person the King was. Maddy seemed cute enough, so perhaps her father wasn't a complete monster. Still, magic could do things to a person, just like money or any other power. All had the liability of corrupting those who held them.

"Why Shirfennelarfin? Why not Jack? Or Patrick?" Aiden asked, voicing a question that had been bugging him for some time.

"Came with the deal he made, I imagine," Kyllena said. "His grandfather's name was Sean McGowan. It's hard to tie a magic to a name like that. It's too common, anyone could take it from you."

Aiden nodded. It made a certain sense, but he was glad he had his wings and a talent for incinerating things that wasn't attached to his name and couldn't be taken away from him.

Torloch arrived much sooner than Aiden would have thought, and the dragon prepared a carefully worded reproach for more safely driving while they had a child in the car. The gargoyle had brought his 2021 Ford Ranger Wolftrak truck, one of the more sensible darlings in his stable.

"I thought about bringing the McLaren," Torloch admitted, correctly reading the expression on his partner's face. "But I doubt it would have impressed Shirfy. And its magnificence is a bit lost in this light."

"Now, what exactly do we do when we get inside?' Aiden asked.

Selena beckoned them over, and showed them a blueprint on her phone. With quick motions and a few words, she outlined their route, and the parts to be especially careful of.

"As you're going through the front door, the most dangerous elements won't be of any concern," she said. "So just make very sure you don't stray from the plan."

"So we take the ballroom-"

"The main one," the vampire said. "It'll be the first one you pass. Not the second, and definitely not the third. If you take the third, you're dumb as rocks and deserve everything that happens to you."

"First ballroom, and then the fireplace back to the fourth-"

"*Fifth*," Selena said. "The fifth one marks the window in the north wall, and your exit."

"Fifth," Aiden repeated, and a trail of smoke curled out as he huffed with concentration.

"Just be aware that you'll be in Shirfennelarfin's private antechamber, so be prepared for anything." A text popped up on the screen, and she swiped it away too fast for Aiden to read anything but *Sandymount* and *make it snappy*. "That should be good enough, it's self explanatory from there. I'm off to take care of a client, a quick lock pick and all that, and I'll head over to help Claudine as soon as I'm done. Won't be long," Selena said with a wave of her hand.

"Thank you, Miss Windbourne," Aiden said with a respectful nod.

"For the love of the goddess, you make me sound like a gray-haired spinster, knitting one of her twelve cats a cardigan," she retorted.

"Don't worry, you're the hottest spinster there ever was," Torloch said.

Selena left with a scowl, and Aiden shrugged at the gargoyle. Torloch had somehow procured a car seat, and Aiden had no idea the gargoyle even knew that such a thing existed, much less where to get one. The gargoyle then expertly put Maddy in the backseat, much to Aiden's shock. Torloch laughed.

"Dude, did you forget how many younger siblings I have?"

Aiden shook his head and turned to the pixie and faery. "We'll meet you by the window in the north wall, just like Selena described," Aiden said, and the pixie nodded.

Before the pixie and the faery disappeared, the dragon pulled Rudy aside. "You keep both eyes on her, and don't blink."

"I won't," the faery promised, and off he went.

The dragon and gargoyle drove through the dark, deserted streets of Dublin, Aiden giving Torloch directions. A short time later, the gargoyle glanced in the rear mirror and frowned.

"What the feck is a guard doing out at this time?" he muttered.

The car pulled up beside him, and a hand waved at them behind the glass.

"Hold on, that's Gordon," Aiden said.

Gordon O'Sullivan was one of the few humans trusted with knowledge of the Fae Realm and was valuable as a go-between for the Outsiders and the Fae. Torloch stopped the car and rolled down his window. The garda stepped out of his vehicle and came around to lean in. He was not in his usual navy and fluorescent yellow uniform, being that he was off duty.

"Good evening boys," he smiled at Aiden and Torloch. "Or should I say good morning?"

He'd only been working with them for about a year, and he was still a little giddy about the idea that he was talking to a dragon and a gargoyle. He was a good sort though, and knew how to keep mum, and just the right thing to say or do to divert awkward questions in tense situations.

"Morning Gordon," Aiden said. "What brings you out at this time?"

"Well, the wife is expecting our second, and was craving some olives and popcorn, so I had to pop out to Spar, to get her a fix," he said.

"Congratulations are in order!" Aiden said.

"Thank you mate," Gordon beamed. "Then I saw a familiar truck, and remembered something. I heard a rather odd story and it just occurred to me, I thought it sounded like you might know what's going on. About one Madeleine McGowan, who happens to be missing at this time."

Maddy giggled at her name, and waved from the back. Aiden and Torloch glanced at each other with an 'oh *shite*' look.

"I just wanted to let you know that your missing kid," Gordon nodded at the backseat without looking directly at her, "is on the Outside news too. I know Sean McGowan's a powerful figure in your world, but he's also known out here. Everyone is on the lookout, and you don't want to be the one caught with her."

"You're not kidding," Adien said. *And you don't know the half of it either.*

"Who the feck is Sean McGowan?" Torloch said grumpily.

"Shirfennelarfin," Aiden said. "I'll explain later. Thanks Gordon. We'll be careful."

"You sure you're alright?" the guard said with a frown. "This seems a bit out of the norm, even for you lot."

"Gordon, we'll buy you a round when we're done," Torloch said. "But don't worry. We know what we're doing. Sort of."

"Well, you know best," the human guard said with a shrug, and stepped back, sending them off with a wave.

Torloch pulled away, and peeled down the streets. Aiden was just about to open his mouth and have that safe driving talk with the gargoyle, when someone else spoke.

"Hello, lads," a dapper voice said from the back seat.

Maddy gurgled happily, and waved the large lollipop that was suddenly in her hand. A well dressed fellow, in a bright red coat and green pants sat in the seat next to her, his leg crossed to show the stylish gold suede boot he wore.

"Who are you?" Aiden said even though he already knew.

"Name's Flynn Farrell," the sharp-eyed man tipped his flat cap with a roguish grin.

He lit a cigarette, and nodded to the left. "Mind opening a window?"

"Do I mind?" Torloch spluttered. "Yes, I mind. Put that out. And get out of my truck!"

"Righto," the far darrig said, and winked out of existence.

Aiden gave a yell.

"What?" the gargoyle said.

"He took her!" Aiden said. "He took Maddy!"

Chapter 11 - Loch

Now I Am Being a Good Boy

Thursday, 20 August 2015, 2:46 A.M. (Dublin)

Loch hit the brakes hard and fast, and he and Aiden were slammed forward before falling back into their seats in stunned silence. Anger crawled down the gargoyle's neck and he knew his eyes had darkened to empty orbs as he put effort into controlling the unusual burst of his unbidden shift.

A far darrig would *not* know how to care for Maddy. All *they* knew how to do was cheat, lie and steal. Without speaking, Loch put the car back in gear and disregarding the heart and stomach of his passenger, he headed to Shirf's domain as quickly as the material world would allow. Aiden stayed quiet the whole way, his silence speaking volumes about how upset he was.

The city roads gave way to country lanes, and when he turned onto the final road from the GPS directions, Loch's carefully controlled emotion began to boil over again in anticipation. Not too long after, the road widened, and became neatly paved and edged with tall hawthorns. The winding drive led to a well-lit security booth outside a set of wide, imposing wrought iron gates. Two stone Sphinx's guarded either side of the entrance, their eyes eerily life-like.

Aiden pressed a hand to Loch's arm. Taking in a very deep, barely-touching-the-surface cleansing breath, Loch turned to look at his partner. He saw a man, a dragon, who cared as much as he did about the child who had fallen into their laps. Forcing his body to relax, Loch gestured at Aiden and then to the window.

"Hello, there," Aiden said jovially as he leaned over Loch to talk to the security guard who had approached the car. "We're here to see King Shirfennelarfin. We're with the Keepers of the Peace and the Order of Chroniclers. We have information about his missing daughter."

"Name?" the burly ogre asked.

"Aiden Moss and Torloch Doyle. Detectives, first class."

The ogre frowned before holding up a finger, the standard sign for 'hang on a minute' and then going back inside the booth. Loch could see him checking a tablet and then picking up a phone.

Loch revved the engine, his fingers itching to throw the gearstick and send the truck crashing through the gate, which was looking more and more flimsy by the second. Not even the menacing looking Sphinxes were enough to deter him.

"Loch, I know what you're thinking, but we really can't go in throwing punches and breaking things to get answers," Aiden said quietly. "At least not on this one. Remember what Selena said about the security? What good are we going to be to Maddy if we're toast?"

Loch scowled. The fury burning inside was threatening to overcome him as he imagined his truck smashing into the little piece of metal that stopped their entry into Shirfy's domain. He took a deep breath, and counted until the fuse disintegrated and Loch calmed. The gargoyle looked at his partner.

"Time to have some fun."

"Torloch-"

"Nope, it's okay. I'm okay." He nodded firmly, and grinned. "I meant once we get through, not now. Now, I am being a *good* boy."

Aiden squinted at his partner but said nothing. The guard finally came out and nodded at them. He pushed a button and the gates swung inward, effectively caging the lion-bodied ladies. Their tails might have twitched, or it might have just been the play of the headlights as the truck moved forwards.

Loch waved and smiled at the guard. "Thank you. Have a nice night!"

They drove up the long and elegantly landscaped drive and parked at the foot of the wide, brightly lit stairway leading to the front entrance of Shirfy's impressive abode. Loch grabbed a satchel from the back seat and swung it over his shoulder, slamming the truck door behind him. The faery lights glowed over the estate grounds, lighting the trees in soft tones as the pair made their way to the palatial home of sandstone, three separate wings and a carriage house big enough for twenty horses visible from the front, and no telling how far it extended back.

A line of ogres, trolls, two giants and an impressively large griffin were lined up before the front doors.

Loch sauntered up to the row of guards. "A grand evening to you all!"

"Actually, it's good morning now," Aiden said.

Loch waved away the technicality, and focused on the creatures in fine livery, who were no doubt more than just decoration or servants. "Who is our escort to visit the illustrious King?"

The two largest trolls stopped forward. One of them was bald and had very large hands. Loch's eyes narrowed briefly before he grinned and nodded. "Excellent! No time to waste then."

"Thank you for your assistance," Aiden offered.

The taller of the two ogres grunted and then turned toward the door gesturing for them to follow. The other ogre stepped in behind them. Loch itched beneath his skin as he carefully took in the details of his surroundings on the walk to meet with Shirfy.

The house was quiet. The sprawling foyer had a grand staircase which Loch assumed would take someone to the personal quarters. The ogre led them to the right, and pushed through a set of extra-tall doors, leading to an empty hallway. The lack of staff made sense considering the early hour.

They walked past an elegant sitting room with a view of the garden. Based on the rows of books, the next room was a library. Loch heard a mumble of appreciation from behind and he turned to roll his eyes at his partner. Aiden pressed his lips together in a grim line making Loch smile.

They were just passing incredibly elegant double doors, rich mahogany accented with gold tracery in the top corners, and large handles in the shape of a dozing crescent moon. Loch stopped abruptly and rubbed his hands together with excitement.

"Dude." He tapped the shoulder of the biggest ogre in front of him. "Is this the *ballroom*?"

The ogre half-turned to glance at the gargoyle, then at the doors, his face scrunched into a distasteful grimace, but he did nod.

Loch pushed toward the door. "I just need a quick peek."

The ogre moved to stop him and Loch saw him glance at Aiden, probably to see if he was going to have a problem. Aiden sighed and spoke.

"Look, if it's not too much trouble, he loves ballroom dancing so much, it really would make his day - erm, night - to see this."

The gargoyle was going to have to have a word with the dragon about his hyper-sensitivity to word choice. Precision in language was one thing, but sometimes Aiden took it too far. Like that "live a very long time" thing about Selena. *So* annoying.

When neither ogre moved, Aiden coughed softly. "And it would be nice to have a personal compliment for King Shirfennelarfin. I'm sure it's a rare event that he has a contender for World Champion Professional Ballroom Dancer in his home. If only he hadn't dipped her so far, and that German hadn't been *quite* so flamboyant with the hand gestures...well, we'll never know what could have been."

The gargoyle kept a straight face through Aiden's fibbing. Watching an eyebrowless ogre raise a brow almost cost Loch his game, but he saved the chuckle for later. In a rare moment of kindness, or perhaps just a hope his boss might think better of him, the ogre pushed open one of the two grand doors. Loch almost felt bad about what was coming. *Almost.*

They walked inside and Loch let out a squeal of delight. Actually, the King's ballroom *was* spectacular, the size of two soccer fields with a marble dance floor taking up three quarters of that space, and the remainder carpeted in a burgundy Pashmina wool. It was easy to imagine the room filled with sparkling lights, gold trim, elegant tapestries and gorgeous figures in dress and costume, spinning and weaving in a magnificent waltz. Aiden's story may have been bullshite, but Loch actually did really enjoy dancing.

As soon as the gargoyle heard the door close, Loch tossed the satchel to the ground. He shredded his shirt as he shifted halfway, while turning and landing a heavy punch into the larger, unsuspecting ogre. He watched as the orge slammed into the ground.

He heard rather than saw Aiden punch the smaller ogre.

Loch looked down at the oaf spread on the floor below him.

"Don't-"

The ogre moved to flip himself upright, but Loch's fist smashed into him again.

"*Ever.*"

The ogre started to move away, and Loch shoved his heavy boot into its gut.

"Hit."

He looked at the dazed ogre as it curled into itself and then lashed out, just missing Loch's face. He almost wished it had hit his stone face.

"My."

The ogre growled and moved so fast with both hands, wrapping them around Loch's neck. Loch growled and slammed his fists into the sides of the ogre's head. It withdrew its hands and bent over in agony. Loch pushed him over.

"Vampire," he spat the last word as the ogre's bloodied head rolled to the side.

"A bit much, don't you think?" he heard Aiden ask, from somewhere behind the red haze of rage. "Took forever."

Loch turned to find Aiden leaning against the wall, next to a finely-woven tapestry, which probably cost more than his house and everything in it, depicting a faery party from some time long forgotten. The smaller ogre was laying on the ground, drool dripping on the rich carpet.

Loch frowned. "Mine was bigger."

"Mhm. And what was that about *your* vampire?"

"Feck off," Loch said, but a smile tugged at the corner of his mouth. It did feel good to say it.

He shifted back to human, grabbed the satchel and pulled a shirt from it, putting it on before slinging the bag over his shoulder again. He followed Aiden over to a mammoth sized fireplace. Aiden studied it for a moment before reaching up to an old gold vase. He pulled it to the right and they both watched in delight as the fireplace turned to the side, showing a passageway in the wall.

"Craic," Loch commented as they walked through the doorway.

"I've always loved these," Aiden agreed.

On the other side, Aiden removed a candle stick from a sconce. The door closed behind them and a fae light bloomed over the candlestick. Since the dragon had listened to the directions and Loch had maybe not as much, mostly because he was distracted by *who* was giving the instructions, Loch let Aiden take the lead, and followed him through the cobwebs and broken stones, past four other sconces.

Pausing, Aiden looked up and found the small window covered with a heavy metal grate. Loch went to his knee and folded his hands together to make a step. Aiden stepped up and reached for the window, flipped open the latch and opened the metal door.

A flash of sparks temporarily blinded him as he heard Kynella's tiny voice.

"Thanks, lads! See you later."

"Wait! Where's Rudy?" Aiden called out in a harsh whisper.

"What am I, his keeper?" the peeved voice of the pixie came. "He had to flitter off to do some Unseelie court thing."

The dragon ground his teeth, and cursed the faery before jumping down. Loch stood and stared back down the hall they had come from.

"Well, she's not very grateful is she?"

Aiden shrugged. "What did you expect of a pixie?"

"At least a kiss," Loch said and chuckled.

Aiden rolled his eyes and continued a few steps down the hall to the fifth sconce. He stopped and looked at Loch in the dim light.

"Ready?"

"After you."

Aiden put the candle into the sconce. The light snicked out of existence and a door slowly moved open, golden firelight spilling into the stone tunnel around them. Aiden rushed through with Loch right behind him.

They had half a moment to inspect the windowless room, the plush carpet, the rich drapes, a shallow pond in the middle, lilies drifting on the placid water, and comfortable furniture sprinkled around the giant antechamber. Everything was edged with gold trim, lace or tassels. The entire room seemed to be designed to wrap a person in a blanket of peace and relaxation, though the handful of KPOC members standing at attention had obviously missed the ambiance. And the gargoyle could hardly blame them.

When his gaze fell on the scene across the room, Loch almost cried. A man he could only suppose was King Shirfennelarfin sat on a throne-like settee, and was bouncing a joyful Maddy on his knee. The King had a long torso and legs wrapped in an elegant royal blue and gold robe. His skin was light, and dark hair curled at his temples. He wore a neat goatee, which only accented the chiseled lines of his face, making them harsh. Maddy gurgled and laughed but to Loch's ears, it didn't sound quite right.

"Detective Doyle and Detective Moss," a very familiar voice no-so-calmly announced their names. "So good of you to join us."

Turning in unison, they were surprised to see Arthur Warren, the leprechaun who headed the Investigation Department of the KPOC, standing just inside the door of the luxurious room. Wild red hair stuck out at all angles, his trousers were crumpled, and his yellow shirt was buttoned unevenly under the tweed jacket, making him look somewhat like he had just rolled out of bed and gotten dressed in the dark, which was probably not too far from the truth.

"Thank you for your assistance, Mr. Warren," the King looked at Aiden as though he'd seen their earlier interactions with his ogres, which he probably had. "Please take them with you when you leave. They're very lucky to be alive."

Loch snorted and could feel Aiden's desire to throttle the gargoyle for his display of bad manners right then.

"Please, King Shirfennelarfin," Aiden said and then bowed. "I beg you to allow me the opportunity to explain."

Loch wanted the opportunity to punch someone's head again but he didn't think that was going to happen. The King considered, stroking his goatee, then he waved a hand, wordlessly instructing Aiden to speak.

Maddy giggled and it irked something in Loch's gut. He pushed it away, figuring he was already missing the kid, and idly scratched his head as Aiden explained the situation with Madame Kynella, her plan and how they came to be bringing him his daughter who vanished from their car. The dragon's voice faltered as his story came to an end, and the antechamber was filled with uncomfortable silence. Shirfennelarfin regarded them with a cold gaze.

"As you can see, your plans have failed. I have my daughter, and that conniving pixie will be caught and dealt with," the King said. "You should be on your way now. To gaol, I think, or at the very least reprimanded and punished *severely*."

Warren neither confirmed or countered the King's judgment and sentence, and Loch balked while Aiden simply shook his head before they started walking toward the stern-faced leprechaun.

"What is the meaning of this?" the King roared.

Hearing a tiny giggle warbling away, Loch turned back and watched as a sparkling streak zipped across the room and vanished. The King was now standing, his fists clenched at his side. And Maddy was nowhere to be seen.

Chapter 12 - Claudine
That Was Not Part Of The Plan

Thursday, 20 August 2015, 4:06 A.M. (Dublin - Headquarters of the Keepers of the Peace and Order of Chroniclers)

C laudine paced her cubicle. It was small, just room for a corner desk, a chair, and a single plant in the far corner - a succulent, dark green vine she'd named Henry. The witch wrung her hands as she waited, and tried to figure out what was happening with the detectives and the child. Had Selena reached them? Had they made it to Shirfennelarfin? Had they been shot out of the sky like Selena had warned them about?

The witch stopped in shock, then shook her head. Nope, not going down *that* path. Her eyes kept sliding to the phone, but it was good that it hadn't rung. That meant they hadn't been caught or needed to throw someone off the trail by misleading them to what Claudine had.

She looked in the corner where her old chair - upholstered in purple, with a daisy-patterned crocheted throw from her grandmother - sat. The copy of Maddy was sleeping peacefully, and Claudine was very glad about this. She had a good idea of what to do with a baby - her half brother Michael was just five, and she'd helped take care of him since he was little - but a magic changeling baby who was actually a pixie? That she didn't really have the first clue about.

She looked at the phone again, then pulled out her cell phone, but no new messages came up. Someone should have done or said something by now. A plaintive cry from the chair banished all thought of the others, and Claudine hurried over. Big blue eyes looked up at her, peeking over the teddy bear Maddy still clutched close to her. Kynella was talented and powerful indeed, to make such a true-to-life copy.

"Wolf?" Maddy asked.

Claudine puzzled at what that meant, shaking her head.

"Den?" the child asked. "Denden?"

"Aiden?" Claudine guessed, and smiled, then frowned.

She knelt in front of the chair and gently smoothed the hair off the child's face. Her skin was very soft, and warm, her brown locks silky smooth. Maddy rearranged her hold on the teddy, and stuck her thumb in her mouth, still looking at Claudine with big eyes. Big eyes that were definitely, absolutely the eyes of a real child.

"Oh dear," the witch said. "This was not part of the plan."

"What's not part of the plan?" a suave voice behind her said, and the witch shrieked in surprise as she spun to see who was talking.

Maddy started to cry, which quickly built into a wail. Claudine scooped her up and gently bounced the child to calm her down, her eyes never leaving the figure in the hallway between cubicles. It was a short, slight man, in a red coat, green pants, and fine gold shoes, with a flat cap and a cigarette. The burning end glinted in his dark eyes as he took a drag, and smiled wider at her.

"Who are you?" the witch asked.

The man tipped his cap. "Flynn Farrell, at your service."

"And what do you want?"

"I'd like to take that child back to her father," he said.

"You're the far darrig," Claudine stated.

"Clever girl," he said, and his smile dropped away. "Now, why don't you hand over the girl, and I'll be on my way?"

The witch took a step back, her eyes darting about to see what she could use as a weapon, or just protection. Her desk was neat - too neat - everything packed away at the end of the work day. Claudine vowed to be less conscientious about mess - a stapler or even a pen could come in handy now.

"How did you get in here?" she asked, stalling for time.

"It wasn't too hard," Flynn Farrell said, and spun around once.

When he turned to face her again, she did not see the neat, dapper man, but the large, somewhat intimidating form of Torloch Doyle. The gargoyle smiled at her, his features almost too dainty for a man, though not unpleasing to look at. Torloch spun, and she once more saw Flynn Farrell. He shrugged.

"It wasn't too hard to convince the security guard that I'd just misplaced my badge, and was coming in to check on you."

"How sweet," Claudine said, taking one last step back, and finding her back up against the wall, as solid and unyielding as the cubicle dividers were flimsy.

"Don't worry," Flynn Farrell said. "I'm really not going to hurt her, or you. I'm just going to take her back to where she belongs. Which is what everybody wants."

The far darrig stepped closer.

Chapter 13 - Aiden
Before Heads Start Rolling

Thursday, 20 August 2015, 4:17 A.M. (Somewhere in Dublin)

Thunder grew on King Shirfennelarfin's face. "Someone had better tell me what is going on *right* now, before heads start rolling."

"I assume you mean that as a figure of speech?" Director Warren spoke up.

The King looked ready to explode, but he pursed his lips, and stood, his fists clenched at his side. "Of course I mean it as a figure of speech. However, my daughter is missing again." He rounded on the dragon and the gargoyle. "Spill. *NOW!*"

"Oh, so now you want to listen to what we have to say? I thought you wanted to throw us in gaol?" Torloch said snidely, and for once, Aiden agreed wholeheartedly with the tone.

Shirfennelarfin spluttered, pointing a shaking finger at them, and then Aiden remembered that he *was* missing his daughter, and pity moved him.

"The child taken from the vampire was a copy," he said. "Maddy is with a far darrig named Flynn Farrell, who has probably brought her to Madame Kynella."

At that moment, a loud 'pop sounded overhead, and a very bedraggled and disheveled Rudy appeared in mid-air, hung there for a moment, and then dropped straight down. If Aiden had not been standing right where he was, the faery would have made a lovely dent in Shirfennelarfin's floor. As it was, Rudy landed neatly in Aiden's arms. The Unseelie prince stared up at the dragon with a groggy smile, his eyes crossing and un-crossing.

"Oh, good, I'm glad you're here," he slurred.

"Rudy, what the *hell* are you doing?" Torloch hissed.

"Who is that?" Warren frowned.

"And *how* did he get in here?" the King added.

Aiden looked at Torloch, beseeching the gargoyle to come up with an acceptable explanation. Rudy, being not only a member of the Unseelie Court, but the son of Queen Mab herself, should have been able to break pretty much any ward.

That was old magic, from the Otherworld. However, he must not have invoked his blood seal, so the King's defenses had battered him around a bit. More than a bit, Aiden thought, looking at the bruises on Rudy's face. How he was going to explain that to his mother was a question for another time. Both the Director and the King were staring at them waiting for an explanation.

"This is...ah, this is-"

"Garvan," Torloch stepped in. "Garvan Murphy. He helps us out from time to time. Friend of my...my..."

"Cousin," Aiden said. "Your cousin Clodagh introduced us. Remember?"

"Right. My lovely cousin Clodagh," Torloch nodded.

The gargoyle didn't *have* a cousin named Clodagh, but no one else needed to know that.

"He was keeping an eye on Kynella," Aiden said, glad to get back on solid ground with the truth.

"Both eyes," Rudy reminded him, the words thick and his eyes still struggling to focus on the dragon's face above him. He reached a hand up and snatched at something in front of Aiden's nose, then looked at his empty hand in confusion.

The dragon sighed. "Can you stand?"

"I think so," Rudy said.

Aiden set him on his feet, but he promptly fell to the left when Aiden let go, and the dragon quickly caught him again.

"Oh, for god's sake," Shirfennelarfin said, and waved imperiously.

A hidden servant hurried forward, and offered Rudy a smoking goblet, crusted with diamonds and rubies. Rudy took it with both hands, sniffed it gingerly, and then gulped down the contents. After a moment, he smiled, and gave a small hiccup. The bruises slowly faded, and his eyes grew bright and clear.

"What was that?" he asked. "It tasted like sunrise, and...dancing."

"The antidote to the ward web you foolishly barrelled through," Shirfennelarfin said, waving the servant away. "Where is this pixie?"

Rudy paled. "Well, the far darrig showed up with Maddy, per the plan."

"What plan?" Aiden said, knowing full well *their* plan had not entailed that *at all*.

"Kynella's plan," Rudy answered, the hint of a whine entering his voice. "I *swear* I didn't know anything about it."

"Go on," the King demanded in a dangerous, cold tone.

"Well, then Maddy, well, she kind of, sort of, wasn't *completely* there any more," Rudy said, stumbling over his explanation. "In fact, she wasn't really there at all. She disappeared!"

Wide-eyed, Torloch looked at Aiden with an expression exactly matching the dragon's feeling, as the two detectives deduced the only logical explanation for what had occurred. They had accidentally taken one of the copies. Which meant the *real* Maddy...

"Claudine," Aiden breathed.

"Who is this?" Shirfennelarfin demanded, his hand raking back through his thick curls in a very agitated gesture.

"A witch," Torloch said. "She works at the KPOC."

"Claudine *Ní Mocháin*?" Warren practically yelled, then took a moment to compose himself before continuing in a more sedate tone. "Exactly who *hasn't* been included in this little scheme?"

"The rest...most of..." Torloch looked at Aiden for help.

"Most of everybody else," the dragon finished. "It's really just us."

"Just you. Of course," Warren said, rubbing the bridge of his nose, then glancing down at his watch. "At four o'clock in the morning."

"What happened after Maddy disappeared?" Shirfennelarfin demanded, looking very much like he wanted to come and shake the rest of the story out of the faery, and Aiden winced as Rudy clung to him a little tighter.

"Kynella wasn't too happy," Rudy said, speaking quickly. "She ate the head off the far darrig for a good minute, then sent him to get the real girl. Then she disappeared as well, and I came to get you."

Through a ward web, Aiden thought, shaking his head. Sometimes Rudy did *not* think things through very well.

"And this Claudine, she has my daughter?" the King asked.

"At Headquarters, the safest place in Ireland, and she's taking very good care of her," Aiden said, hoping that was true.

"Well?" the King roared, rounding on Warren. "Why aren't you doing something about that?"

"Move it people! Let's *go!*" the Director shouted at the KPOC team as he spun on his heel to make for the door, driving everyone to action.

Shirfennelarfin followed, his polished boots clicking crisply down the marble halls of his home, as the agents jogged behind him to keep us. Warren grabbed Aiden and Torloch's shoulder and jerked them back.

"I swear, if this turns out badly, both of you are going to answer to me personally," the leprechaun said through gritted teeth. "I do *not* need this right now!"

It wasn't *very* fair of him, given the more or less exemplary history of the outcomes of their cases (though the middle bits could get a bit messy), but the Director was under a lot of stress, and it was four o'clock in the morning, as he has pointed out.

"Yes, sir," Aiden said, hoping Torloch kept his mouth shut.

Outside, a light rain had started to mist down. A caravan of cars pulled out of Shirfennelarfin's drive, onto the small road to Dublin city. As fast as Torloch had driven to the King's palace, he was not driving fast enough for Aiden right now. To be fair, that had more to do with the car in front of them, containing Warren and the King, but still.

"What the hell happened?" the dragon asked.

"The witch must have been mistaken," Torloch said.

"Or Kynella tricked her," Aiden said. "Either way, we have to get there five minutes ago."

"We should really be flying," Torloch said through gritted teeth. "We'd be there in a flash."

"Right, and Warren was going to agree to that in the state he's in," Aiden said, glancing ahead at the red lights shining through the rain.

The convoy picked up speed on the deserted Chesterfield Ave through Phoenix Park, and squealed into the hidden car park of Headquarters. Brendan the security guard blinked as they ran past him without bothering to flash their badges, doing a double take when he saw Torloch.

"But..but Detective Doyle," the ogre at the front desk started to say, blinking as he tried to work out how to finish the statement, but the gargoyle was already past, running down the hall after Aiden and a surprisingly fast Warren.

"Ms. Ní Mocháin's cubicle is on the second floor, back offices," Warren said, waving team members ahead of him.

"Seems a shame to keep such a pretty face hidden there," Torloch said.

"Doyle," Warren's warning tone fell slightly flat on his huffing and puffing. He was speedy, but he wasn't exactly in his prime either.

They turned the corner to the first floor of the Primary Offices, sprinted to the end and up the four flights of stairs to the second floor. The office was dark, only one light remained on in the far back corner, and they saw a smallish figure wearing a familiar red coat in the doorway of the cubicle.

Chapter 14 - Loch
I Have a Fear of Missing Out

Thursday, 20 August 2015, 4:51 A.M. (Dublin - Headquarters of the Keepers of the Peace and Order of Chroniclers)

Everything happened very quickly. The far darrig bolted as the KPOC members flew toward him. He may not have been able to evaporate into thin air due to the wards of the KPOC but he sure as feck was fast. Loch thought of himself as a swift runner, and it was true he was no slouch, but the gargoyle was like a lumbering four-year-old as he gave chase.

Aiden was more nimble and agile but even he was breathing heavily to keep the annoying fae in sight. Warren and Shirfy were far behind as they followed along at ridiculous speeds through the hallways and toward the front door.

"Brendan!" Aiden shouted as they neared the front entrance.

The security guard must have jumped into action within half a second, as he appeared at the end of the hallway with his baton in one hand and balled fist in the other. Taking in the situation barrelling toward him in a rapid glance, he held up his baton and fired two bolts of immobilizing mage fire at the runaway, the shining balls of purple and green narrowly missing the little man in the red coat, spinning over his shoulder to splatter harmlessly against the stone wall behind him.

The far darrig put on a burst of speed, and launched himself into the air, vaulting over the ogre with an ease that had a few choice words roll from Loch's gasping mouth. Ahead of them, the front doors began to open from the other side. Someone was coming in!

"No!" Both Loch and Aiden yelled as someone stepped through, and they skidded to a halt and watched the beauty before them.

The speed with which the newcomer came through the door was such a blur that Loch wouldn't have recognized who it was, save the glorious scent of vanilla and sugar cookies. By the time they were all full stop, Selena had the far darrig hanging in the air, her hand clasped around his jaw.

In a moment of celebratory exuberance, Loch stepped forward and pressed a kiss to the vampire's cheek. She frowned at him, and he was suddenly aware of how reckless that was, but she did no more than look at him for a moment longer and shake the far darrig impatiently.

"Thanks, love," he said and gave her a cheeky grin before grabbing Flynn Farrell by his one arm.

Aiden took his other arm and once convinced he would not be getting away, Selena released the fae to their care.

"Get a cuff on him," Warren ordered when he finally caught up a few moments later, a slight limp making his gait uneven. "Quickly now." he nodded at Selena. "Just in time, thank you."

She shrugged it off with a slight smile, and held up a manila folder marked "Confidential". "I was in the neighborhood, just dropping this off before I dropped in to see Claudine."

She strode by, and winked at Loch before moving along to the security services with her accounting.

Brendan moved quickly and slipped the cuff around the faery's ankle. Any chance of him getting out the door and vanishing had just been removed by the spelled metal. The boys turned Flynn over to Brendan as another guard came in the front door.

"Hello, Harry," Aiden nodded to the guard, a reedy wizard with gold-rimmed spectacles.

He didn't look like much, but he was a welter-weight boxing champion, and had a mean roundhouse kick. He was also something of a mixologist and could whip up a wonderful Irish coffee.

"Hello, sir," the wizard nodded at the dragon. "Turns out I have a fear of missing out."

Loch snorted and patted the man on the shoulder as he beckoned toward the far darrig. "I'm sure Brendan would love an extra hand with this one."

Harry happily joined the ogre and they departed, escorting the bad guy to his gaol cell. Loch watched King Shirfennelarfin stride towards the front door, passing the guards in the hall with barely a glance as he made noises unbefitting of a king to the cheerful little girl in his arms.

Claudine walked sedately just behind them, moving to stand next to Warren. Loch heard a whispered offer of a healing tincture, and the gargoyle managed to keep a straight face as Warren tried to politely decline the foul concoction.

"I want to thank you all for helping to bring my daughter back to me. She is my pride and joy." The King turned and smiled gratefully at everyone, faltering only slightly at the gargoyle and dragon.

Loch wanted to roll his eyes. Sometimes you have to know what you've done right and leave it at that. Maddy started to wriggle in his arms, trying to escape his embrace, and the King let her down. He watched like a hawk as Maddy toddled over to Aiden and smiled up at him.

"Denden," she said and blew him a sloppy kiss.

Aiden bent down and patted her on the head with a fond smile. Claudine might have *oohed* slightly. King Shirfy decided his child wasn't in any danger, and he stepped over to have a word with Warren, as Maddy moved to Loch. The gargoyle let out a low growl, making a funny face. Everyone's eyes moved to him, like he was doing something bad and the King started to step forward. Maddy only giggled and wrapped her arms around Loch's left leg briefly.

"Wolfy. Bye wolfy," she said before letting go and running back to her father.

The child paused when Claudine came into view, and veered around the King and raised her hands to the witch.

"Up!" Maddy demanded.

Blinking back a little water from her eyes, Claudine reached down and lifted the child into a hug before handing her back over to her father. He held her like the delicate treasure she was, nodded at Loch and Aiden with maybe the hint of an extra acknowledgement, and walked out of the building. The entire room seemed to sink back to earth, several sighs of relief were had, Loch included.

Loch looked at each person and bowed to the room, feeling that something needed to be said to mark the end of this adventure. "May your day be touched with a bit of Irish luck, Brightened by a song in your heart, And warmed-"

"Go home, Torloch," Warren ordered gently.

"Yes, sir," the gargoyle was not going to argue. "You coming, A?"

"Be right out."

Loch was pretty certain that Aiden needed a word with Claudine and he certainly couldn't begrudge him that. He walked out the door and found Selena walking silently next to him.

"Thanks for the epic stealing of our show," he commended.

"Right place, right time," she said dismissively.

"Still a sight to behold."

The vampire looked at him for a long time, and it was hard to read what was behind her dark eyes. He wondered if he had been too forward, too fast, and he mentally kicked himself, but then he saw the slightest softening of her expression, and a faint twinkle in her gaze.

"Back atcha, gargoyle."

Loch wanted to say more. He didn't know what he should say exactly, but he desperately wanted to keep talking to her. However, it was not to be, and she flashed him a shy grin and ran off at vampire-speed, to the parking lot. He watched her get into her Audi S8, a beautiful, deep purple color with almost black tinted windows to guard her from the sun in case she got stuck out during the day. The car roared to life, and the red brake lights faded as she peeled away.

The gargoyle smiled as he got into his Wolftrack, Aiden joining him moments later.

"And now, a snack and *sleep*," Loch commented as they drove out of the parking lot toward home and bed.

He spared a moment to greet his rabbits and the cat, and then crashed into blissful sleep. Several hours later Loch woke feeling rested and even more happy. He wondered if last night had been a dream, but the first tiny stitch of mending in his shattered heart told him there was hope. His phone dinged on the side table and he glanced at the message and grinned.

He went into the kitchen for breakfast, eh, lunch at this point and was happy to find Aiden already at work, surrounded by milk, flour, a huge mound of grated cheese, and a pile of vegetables. Loch slid into a chair at the table, his striped Maine Coon cat jumping onto the table and blinking blue eyes expectantly at him. Loch scratched around his ears as Aiden spoke.

"Before turning in last night, I was able to brine the pork chops, and they turned out *so* well. I'm making lunch now, with Gnocchi Mac and Cheese and a Roasted Vegetable Medley. Should be ready in a few minutes." He smirked at the gargoyle. "If you can wait that long."

"I thank the goddesses every day that your chefness has deigned to find my west wing habitable," Loch said, practically frothing at the mouth in excitement for his midday meal.

Aiden continued speaking as he made magic happen in the kitchen, sprinkling nutmeg and garlic in the cheese sauce, and expertly sautéeing the vegetables in olive oil. "I found out this morning that King Shirfennelarfin caught Madame Kynella and was going to put her in his dungeon."

"No way!"

"*But...*" Aiden paused to taste the sauce he was stirring in the cast iron pan, then continued his story. "*Rudy* of all people showed up - through the front door this time, I believe - and between his defense of Kynella's intentions, and Maddy's affectionate greeting of the pixie, they convinced the King to allow her the wish *and* to leave without even a single night in his dungeon."

"Really? He didn't seem all that nice of a guy last night."

"Well, in his defense, it was the wee hours of the morn and his daughter was missing." Aiden looked over. "Truthfully, how cheerful would you be if your cat was missing?"

"Fair point," Loch nodded as he poured himself a cup of tea.

He took a soothing sip before drumming the table, wondering how to tell the dragon the good news.

Aiden glanced at him. "What?"

Loch's eyes lit up. "Guess where we're going in just a few short hours?"

The dragon raised a brow and narrowed his eyes slightly.

"Prepare yourself for the incredible, the amazing, *the once of a lifetime opportunity* to see a live performance..."

Aiden paused in stirring a dish that Loch knew would make his taste buds sing, a wide grin spreading over his face. "We're finally going to see Uaithne?"

"Yep! The show was delayed by the weather, the warlocks couldn't keep up, and so it works out perfectly to celebrate yet another case closed."

"I don't think that was technically a *case*."

"Sure it was."

"No, not really, not a proper *case* case. We simply found a girl and went about locating where she belonged-"

"A, can we just enjoy the craic, *without* arguing about definitions for once?"

Aiden pressed his lips together, but his smile broke through. "Yes, Torloch. As soon as you move that cat from the table, lunch is ready."

Epilogue
Just Under 7 Years Later

Friday, 27 May 2022, 9:17 PM (Dublin, Ireland)

The banshee's scream cut through the evening, sending chills crawling over the dragon's skin even though the sound was only a recording, coming through small but expensive-looking speakers hidden behind the large bush in the park.

"Hey, look at this!" Torloch called from a few feet away. "I found her!"

Aiden stood up, brushing dirt off his knees, then straightening. The gargoyle held up a switch, and then flicked it on. An image of a woman in a black mourning veil flickered to life just behind the tree, somewhat like the princess Leia projection in Star Wars. Torloch turned the switch off, and the "banshee" disappeared.

"So that's how he's doing it," Aiden murmured. "Clever little con man."

"Evil little shite, you mean," Torloch corrected. "Scaring people to death is *not* a nice thing to do."

"Technically, he only scared them out of their money," the dragon said. "No one has died."

"Do you know how much I hate it when you say *technically*?" the gargoyle complained. "Mostly because of what follows *that* word."

"Well, now we've got the means," Aiden said. "All that's left is to catch him."

"*All* that's left," Torloch rolled his eyes.

"Hey!" Aiden protested. "This is the closest we've gotten to him in a month!"

"You're right," the gargoyle said. "Nice interrogation on that last guy we brought in. Perfectly executed."

Now it was Aiden's turn to roll his eyes. "It wasn't an *interrogation*, it was an interview, which might be why you missed that he said he saw the banshee when eating lunch for the past few days. All I did was ask him where he eats lunch."

"I'll have you know that I've had a great deal of success with my particular brand of interro-views, thank you very much," the gargoyle said.

A faint pop and a muted shower of hazy lavender sparks showered over them, as Rudy surreptitiously appeared.

"Guys, guys, guys!" he hissed in a voice that Aiden swore was loud enough to be heard across the park, but maybe that was just nerves. "He's coming! He's on his way here!"

With that, the faery disappeared again, to *where* the dragon didn't know. There was no point returning to his look-out post, and unless the Unseelie prince had developed the skill of clairvoyance in the last fifteen minutes, he couldn't be going to where he would be needed - namely, where their suspect would run and take cover.

"Well, he'll be able to tell that someone's discovered his hiding place," Torloch said, looking around at the trampled bushes and scuffed grass.

"So I guess we're working on a Friday night again," Aiden said, mostly just to annoy the gargoyle, and was rewarded with a half-sulky look.

A moment later, a figure came into view, and resolved into Harlow Faulkner sauntering from around a nearby tree. He stopped and looked at them, a deer-in-the-headlights expression, then dropped the boxes he carried and bolted away. Torloch cursed, and immediately gave chase. Aiden put in a call to Headquarters, knowing he didn't have to worry about the guy getting away.

The gargoyle may not have been as good at interrogation as he thought he was, but he sure as feck could run like the wind.

*****

For more adventures of Aiden the Dragon and Torloch the Gargoyle, click here to get *A Dragon, a Gargoyle, and a Faery Walk into a Pub,* the first book in the series!

To join our *free community on REAM stories click here!*

For more about Nicole DragonBeck (the voice of Aiden Moss) click here!

For more about Lisa Barry (the voice of Torloch Doyle) click here!

www.ingramcontent.com/pod-product-compliance
Lightning Source LLC
Chambersburg PA
CBHW070600180626
46817CB00005B/1931